WINTER'S HEART

J.E. Taylor

Winter's Heart © 2019 J.E. Taylor

Cover Art by julienicholls.com

WINTER'S HEART

Myths. Magic. And a prophecy realized.

Lisa Winters is supposed to save the small town of Opal from destruction with magic she does not possess. The white tiger has awoken, and he wants revenge on the people who betrayed him, as well as the sorceress who bound him in frost.

Lisa was not that witch. And yet, everyone believes she is the fated one. The one who will finally end the white tiger's reign of terror.

Even her mentor, Herk, thinks so.

Lisa doesn't want to let anyone down, but she can barely start a fire with a match and lighter fluid, let alone do anything magical.

That is, until the moment she meets the white tiger.

His majestic beauty stirs deep within her soul. Her magic, dormant for so long, sparks to life like a shooting star streaking across the universe.

But as the burst fades, so does her strength, leaving her vulnerable to the tiger's wrath.

Chapter 1

"TRY AGAIN!" HERK CANICULA stood over Lisa like a handsome and frightening tyrant. His dark hair blew in the cold breeze, and his grey eyes looked like the ice on Opal Lake. But his demand was futile. He might as well have asked for the last drop of her blood.

"I am!" she cried, concentrating until sweat dripped into her eye, stinging.

She closed her hands and slumped on the sitting log around the great circle of fire. Except there was no fire. It was as cold as she was. She couldn't even light a damn candle with her mind, never mind light it like the prophets foretold.

She had no magic.

Not even a flicker, despite Herk's insistence that she did. She hadn't possessed it since she was a small child, and she was convinced that had not been actual magic.

The one time that she had, it was because she had gotten so mad at her parents, angry enough for sparks to snap from her fingertips. They were in a public place with enough people to start hearing murmurs about her being *that* girl. It wasn't long after that incident that a fire took all that she knew and loved and Herk's family took her in.

"This is a waste of time, and you know it. I haven't created magic since I was four, if that's even what it was." They went through this daily. This exact argument every single day since she'd turned eighteen. He hadn't left her any time for friends or fun, and she was tired. Tired of this same stale routine.

"Which is why we have been trying to help you tap into it ever since," he said and leaned his hands on the table next to her. "You've been able to move things with your mind before," he added. It was his way of coaxing her into continuing.

Telekinesis was very different than magic, but she wasn't going to argue with him. She could almost repeat this lecture word for word at this point. Two years of failed practices and Herk's bullying her into exhaustion. He seemed to think she was the fabled one who would beat the white tiger if it ever awoke from its long winter slumber.

The mountains buffered Opal from the rest of the world, and they were content in their little snow-filled region, so she didn't understand why parents continued to scare their children with the stories about the white tiger's return and the inevitable slaughter.

It was just a story.

She closed her eyes, and instead of willing the candle lit, she wished Herk would just give her a day of solitude and rest. This was not the way to get her mind to open. A lazy day in bed with a good book was all she needed. But that would never come to pass.

Not with Herk and his obsession.

"You can do this," he said softly, trying to coax the magic out of her.

She opened a single eyelid and stared up at him, determined to change this mundane routine of his. "I need rest. You do know the entire idea of insanity is repeating things every day and expecting a different outcome."

His lips thinned and his glare sharpened. "You think I'm insane?"

She sighed. So much for the ability to change his crazy pattern. She did not want to have words with him. Not with exhaustion licking every muscle to the point she thought she would just slide off the seat into a writhing puddle of goo.

"I am going to do something more useful than staring at a candle wick for the next six hours and expecting it to spontaneously combust." She stood.

"Sit down," he bellowed in her face and drew back as if he were going to strike her.

"No!" For the first time in years, she stood her ground and didn't flinch as the muscles in his arms tightened. "And if you so much as lay a finger on me, I will break it." She was in no mood to be bullied beyond exhaustion today. She'd had enough of his sick game.

Instead of backhanding her, he wiped his face and closed his eyes. She could almost see his mental pep-talk to rein in his anger. When he opened his eyes, they still held the dark grey of frustration, but there was something else underneath. Something more feral, like she had just ruined a much-anticipated date.

He inhaled and then nodded. "Fine. Let's head inside, and I'll make you a nice hot cup of our special tea."

"You know what? I am not in the mood for tea right now. What I need is a walk." She started towards the path, and when Herk fell into step by her side, she glared at him. "Alone."

Hurt flared in his eyes, but she was past the point of worrying about his fragile ego. All he wanted was her to save the day. To produce magic as easily as snapping her fingers. Magic that had only surfaced once, and if there was anything the years following that strange release of magic had taught her, that sorcery had been a fluke.

Chapter 2

THE BLANKET OF WHITE covering the forest floor calmed her as much as the cool breeze. Lisa knew Herk wasn't her enemy, but since she'd turned eighteen, his obsession had changed him into someone she didn't know. She wouldn't have guessed her oldest, dearest friend could become such a vicious slave driver.

She had once told him she didn't feel worthy of all the attention. She wasn't a mystical goddess who could stop Opal from destruction.

She couldn't even stop water from boiling over in a pot.

He had been so determined to prove her wrong. That was what drove him to these daily practice sessions. She wondered if she had kept her thoughts to herself, would he have become this demanding tyrant?

She shook her head and drifted farther into the woods where the pines thickened, blanketing the snow with needles and sap. It smelled glorious, and she took a deep inhalation through her nose letting the evergreens fill her senses.

Something shifted in her peripheral vision, but when she looked, nothing was there. Perhaps snow had just slipped off a branch. She scanned the area, but nothing marred the perfect landscape.

Her skin tingled, and she glanced around, turning in a circle as the overwhelming sensation of being watched interrupted her peaceful walk. A plume of steam escaped from her lips with a deep sigh.

She turned, heading back to the village before the sun dipped below the mountain ridge and the icy winds picked up. She did not want to get caught in the deep woods in the dark. There were bears and wolves and other sordid creatures that came out after the sun set to hunt.

And she had been thoughtless enough to leave without any decent weapon.

Lisa hurried along, still feeling the heat of eyes on her, but when she glanced back, only white painted the ground. She slowed to a stop and stood still for a full minute, trying to shake the weird sensation.

She turned back towards the village. Snow shifted and fell in a great chunk, plopping onto the snow-covered ground, making her jump. The winds were picking up, and she quickened her pace, hell-bent on outrunning the coming gales.

A blast of warmth welcomed her along with hushed conversation as she stepped inside the Caniculas' house. Herk peeked around the kitchen doorway, his worried brow smoothing at the sight of her.

"I have some hot tea for you," he said.

She hated the tea they plied her with at least once a day. It tasted like charcoal with a hidden bitterness and always made her hands feel heavy. This tea had become a staple in her life ever since she'd moved in with them. And she didn't have the heart to tell Mrs. Canicula just how awful her home-brewed tea really was.

"I'm still not in the mood for tea," she said and headed towards the stairs.

"The tea will revitalize you," Mrs. Canicula said from just beyond Herk. "Come. Sit. While it's still hot." She poked her head out from behind Herk with that warm smile Lisa couldn't turn down.

She resigned herself to their imposed routine. "Fine. But just a half cup tonight." She didn't want to be up at midnight with her mind racing. The hideous-tasting tea seemed to strip her of the ability to sleep, which made concentrating for Herk's training sessions especially draining.

She sat down and steeled herself as Mrs. Canicula placed a steaming full cup in front of her. Lisa sighed and picked it up. She had tried to burn her taste buds many times to drown out the taste, but that hadn't worked. Neither had loading the cup with sugar.

There was no escaping this, so she blew on the steam then closed her eyes and quickly drank the cup, ignoring the burn that traveled all the way down her esophagus. She shivered as it plunged into her stomach like a lead ball. Her eyelids shot up as the heat hit, but she didn't make a noise. She crossed to the sink and turned on the cold water, leaned over, and gulped enough to staunch the fire in her mouth.

When she straightened and turned, the family was staring at her. Granted, she hadn't done that in years.

She shrugged. "I guess I was thirstier than I thought." She let out a nervous laugh and forced a yawn. "I'm going to head upstairs for a bit."

She went through her normal bedtime routine, brushing her hair until it shone, polishing her teeth, and rinsing the dirt and grime off her face. By the time she slipped into bed, her limbs had that heavy feeling the tea always seemed to bring.

Just as her eyelids started their slow descent, a soft knock pulled her from the edge of sleep. She groaned and glanced at the door.

Herk poked his head inside. "Can I come in?" he asked with eyes so full of concern that Lisa nodded.

He crossed and took a seat on the edge of the bed. "Are you okay?"

She sighed. "I'm just tired. Tired of our grueling days of no progress. Tired of the way the townspeople stare at me as if I'm some new revelation that was delivered from God. I'm just tired." Lisa threw her arm over her eyes before he caught the sudden mist of emotion that threatened.

"I get it, but if you're going to stop the white tiger when he wakes—"

"*If* he wakes. If he even exists." She sat up and glared at him. "This is all fables and folklore. It's not based in reality."

"Then marry me," he said.

Lisa opened her mouth to argue, and then his words settled in. She blinked at him like he'd just asked her to slit her own wrists. "What?"

His lips tilted in a half grin. "Marry me."

There were so many women in Opal who fawned over Herk, but he didn't seem interested in any of them. Even Lisa's friends at school would have gladly lain with him if he had shown interest. But Lisa had never seen him as anything but an older brother, which was the only reason she let him treat her so harshly day after day. Not once, even in her wildest dreams, did she ever envision a romantic entanglement with him.

As a matter of fact, just the thought soured her stomach, threatening to purge the tea still sitting like a rock in her belly.

"No." She pushed herself back against the headboard, putting as much distance between them as possible. Nothing about being with Herk romantically settled right.

Herk's brow creased, and his arms flexed as tight as his jawline. He stood and marched out of the room without another word.

Chapter 3

THE NEXT MORNING, LISA dragged herself out of bed, disoriented and achy from sleeping so deeply that the entire village of Opal could have been slaughtered and she wouldn't have woken to the screams.

She rubbed her face and headed into the bathroom.

She met her blue-grey gaze in the mirror as she studied her mussed-up hair. The shine from last night had faded into a rat's nest from sleep.

She threw water on her face to lift the fog from her brain.

Herk had asked her to marry him? She blinked at her image, trying to decipher if it had been a dream or not. She couldn't be sure based on the stupor she had gone to bed in.

Lisa brushed her teeth as she mulled it over in her mind. The more she polished, the more she questioned whether it had happened. No way. Herk had never so much as made a pass at her.

Even as kids, he had a gruff way about him, like he was trying to not resent her for being in their home. He never handled her like she was a breakable piece of china. Until she turned eighteen, he would slide into her room to talk late at night after everyone in the house had gone to bed. He'd told her his dreams. His plans for Opal and beyond. And in none of those nightly conversations had he ever expressed wanting a future with her. And he certainly never made a move, and god knows he'd had plenty of opportunity.

They had been friends, confidants, more like siblings. She must be confusing a dream with reality.

By the time she stepped into the kitchen, she had herself convinced. It wasn't until Herk didn't even acknowledge her that her doubts evaporated. The glare he gave her before he stormed away all but screamed it at her.

"Why?" she blurted before he exited the kitchen.

He stiffened in the doorway but didn't turn.

"Because maybe I can help you attain your destiny," he muttered and marched off.

She didn't know what she expected him to say, but making it sound more like a business arrangement rather than a romantic tryst made it all the more unappealing. The man she married would be the one to sweep her off her feet. He would make her see fireworks when he kissed her, and he would be much kinder and gentler than Herk had ever been.

She slammed her cereal bowl down on the kitchen table and focused on eating, but it did nothing to calm the storm brewing inside. When she stepped outside to the start of another grueling day of training, Herk was nowhere to be found. Neither were her neighbors.

She crossed to the road and looked towards the center of town. People were gathered around the great hall. Even from this distance, a woman's cry reached her from within the crowd.

Lisa started towards the group slowly at first, but the continued wail quickened her footsteps.

She pushed her way to the front and stopped short at the gruesome scene.

The town constable crouched next to one of the older women in town who was holding the dead body of her husband. Great swaths of torn flesh crisscrossed his abdomen and face. She would have guessed he was mauled by a bear until she saw the bloody footprints in the snow.

Four-toed paw prints. Two bloodied, and two pristinely cast in the snow. Bear prints have five toes and longer claws.

She looked up at Herk on the other side of the circle. His hard glare was on Lisa. Soon, everyone else's attention was on her as well.

"The white tiger has risen," he said.

A chill caught Lisa, and she wrapped her arms around her to stop her from actually shivering. It was bad enough Herk was staring at her, but now the widow and the rest of the town had started to notice that Lisa was present as a witness to this massacre.

"It appears that way," Constable Jones said and stood, looking at Lisa as if she had suddenly become this town's savior.

Now she wished she had stayed in bed and not bothered with starting her day. This was worse than finding out Herk had really proposed to her. Worse yet, the town expected her to magically make this tiger disappear. They expected her to fulfill the prophecy.

Herk crossed and grabbed her arm, leading her out of the crowd and back towards his training grounds before any other of the townspeople started to join in with 'what are you going to do about this' looks.

She was grateful for the exit until Herk opened his mouth again.

"It's time to tap that magic."

Was he serious? The last thing she wanted to do was stare at a cold fire for another eight hours.

"I beg to differ. It's time for me to wield a sword or pick up my bow." She yanked her arm from his grip. "If we are going to war with the white tiger, don't you think I should be able to defend myself? Or are you hoping that I'll be the next victim?"

He skidded to a halt and glared at her, pointing his finger accusingly. "You are destined to kill that thing. And magic is the only thing that can kill that beast."

"Bullshit. It's just a tiger. I can't even make sparks appear on my fingertips, never mind blast that thing back to where it came. I need to start practicing with either my bow or a sword."

"Only magic can defeat him." He crossed his arms. "Or are you missing that point."

Lisa threw her hands into the air. There was no reasoning with Herk. The lore was just as full of crap as his insistence she was *that* girl. "Then we are all screwed, because I don't possess magic," she argued much louder than she intended.

A throat cleared behind them, and they spun to see the village secretary. He adjusted his glasses and looked off at the thick woods at the edge of town.

"The council would like to speak with you," he said to Lisa.

"Tell my father I will be there in a minute," Herk said.

"I wasn't talking to you," the man said. "Your father has requested Miss Winters presence before the council."

"Oh," Herk mumbled, and his cheeks reddened. He waved Lisa to follow the village secretary.

She raked her hand through her hair and nodded, following him down the street with Herk a few steps behind like some morbid protection detail, or an escort walking her to her death.

Chapter 4

LISA WALKED INTO THE Opal hall of council, and everyone around the table stood as if she were royalty. She shifted under their worried gazes. Silence weighed on her like a heavy blanket as suffocating as their stares.

"What do you plan to do?" Randolph Canicula, the head of the council, asked. His brazen gaze left Lisa uncomfortable. And not just because he was the head of the council. It was because Randolph was Herk's father, and he had to have known Lisa turned his son's proposal down. Why else would he pin this responsibility on her?

"Excuse me?" Lisa balked and shuffled her feet. She had no answers. She had no magic to protect Opal. She only had her sword and bow, which she hadn't picked up since she'd turned eighteen and Herk started his insane training sessions. She was not prepared for the weight of the duty being thrust upon her.

"You are the chosen one. It is your destiny to rid Opal of this white tiger business." He leaned forward, pointing at her as if accusing her of killing that man herself.

"I am not the chosen one," she snapped. "I don't have any magic, and I have been trying to tell you that for years!"

A hush fell over the council, and they traded worried glances. That is, everyone except Randolph. His glare was as unnerving as the silence. When his glare moved behind her, she glanced over her shoulder at Herk still standing in the doorway.

He shrugged in a non-committal way that suddenly made Lisa's blood boil. Like he didn't care that she hadn't shown signs of magic since she was four years old. It was as if her magic had been a premonition of sorts. Days after her fingers sparked flame, her home burned to the ground with her parents inside. Lisa had not been home that day. Otherwise, she would have perished, too.

She had been at the Caniculas' house for Herk's thirteenth birthday party along with the lion share of the town's children.

"You are the chosen one," Randolph snarled. "And you will remove the danger of the white tiger from Opal, even if you have to spill your own blood to do so."

He definitely knew. Otherwise, he wouldn't have sentenced her to a sure death.

"Father." Herk's voice held a dark warning that even she couldn't ignore.

"I can fight my own battles," she said, putting her hand up to silence whatever argument Herk might launch into in front of the high council of Opal. Whatever it was, she was sure he was about to embarrass her in some way, like tell the council she would get mortally wounded if she was the one to hunt the white tiger, or something equally as mortifying.

His huff of derision jarred her enough for her teeth to ache while she gnashed them together.

"I will do my best," she said to the council. "But understand, I am not your magical chosen one. Regardless, it seems you are adamant that I be the one to hunt the monster, so I will go out there with my bow and my quiver and shoot the tiger in the eye."

"Lisa," Herk said softly from behind her. His voice was laced with something she had never heard from him. It sounded a bit like fear.

She turned and stormed past him, leaving the town hall in a march that had her footfalls echoing. The cold slapped at her cheeks as she stepped outside. She didn't even know where Herk had put her weapons. At least before she was eighteen, he had trained her with a bow and a sword, but it had been a couple years since she'd wielded a weapon.

Either way, she was on her own to take care of the beast.

That thought sobered her, and even though her feet wanted to falter, she forced her steps to continue, even with the crunch of hurried footsteps behind her.

A hand gripped her arm and spun her around.

"You aren't ready," Herk said. His eyes were a little more frantic now that the gauntlet had been dropped on her.

Lisa yanked her arm from his grip. "You heard them." She pointed at the building they had just vacated. "They expect me to take care of this with or without magic."

"I'm going with you," he said.

That's all she needed. While Herk was an experienced fighter, he hadn't trained with a sword or a bow either. Instead, he'd put all his bets on her magic and drilled her relentlessly daily.

"No." She didn't need his death on her hands, too. Besides, she had been the better archer out of the two of them. Although, he could beat her black and blue with a training sword.

His jaw tightened and his nostrils flared. He glanced at the woods in the distance. "Then at least let me train with you a little. It's been a while since you held a weapon."

She looked down at her feet, debating. The last time she'd sparred with Herk, he'd left her almost as exhausted as the daily practice of unsuccessful magic. She didn't know if she could go after a tiger with that kind of grueling test.

"Are you trying to ensure I will not return?" she finally asked. Her voice was filled with every ounce of aggravation burning through her bones.

He stepped back, and she looked up at his face. Horror stretched his eyes wide, and she immediately regretted her question.

"No. How can you say that after I asked you to marry me last night? Your death... will devastate me," he said.

Will? Like he expects me to die? What the ever-loving hell?

Lisa's head nearly exploded with anger, and the red hue covering her vision didn't help. She spun and marched away, muttering foul words under her breath. Even Herk had crossed her off. Now she was even more determined to drag back the carcass of the dead tiger, just to show this town that she was not to be trifled with in the future.

Chapter 5

"YOU NEED TO GO to the funeral and pay your respects," Herk said from the doorway.

His voice held a cool warning that Lisa had no intention of obeying. She didn't need to go to a funeral to be motivated to do her duty. What she needed to do was hone her skills with her bow and arrow, but she didn't want Herk's help with that.

When Mrs. Canicula poked her head in behind Herk, her warm expression hardened. "You're not ready yet?"

"No, ma'am. I'm not feeling well." Lisa didn't like how easily the lie rolled off her tongue, but she needed to be alone. She had every intention of packing up and heading into the mountains to find the tiger as soon as everyone left for the funeral. While her skills with a bow might be rusty, she had been the best shot in Opal when she was younger.

She just hoped her steady hand wouldn't fail her. Otherwise, hers would be the next funeral this town would see.

Besides, she knew deep down that Herk would follow her if she left while he was around. And she didn't want that. He would drive her as relentlessly as he had in his training sessions, and she did not need that type of pressure.

"You need to suck it up and come with us," Mrs. Canicula said. "I'll make you some tea while you get dressed." She turned and left the room, leaving Lisa no choice but to obey the unrelenting command in her tone.

Lisa closed her eyes and tilted her head back. Escaping wasn't going to happen today, and she would just have to plan to sneak out at another time. Begrudgingly, she waved Herk out of the room and put on proper clothing for a funeral. Her wool leggings matched her dark wool skirt and her black lace-up boots that put her almost at Herk's height. Her sweater pulled the grey in her eyes to the forefront, muting the blue. She smoothed her skirt and made her way downstairs where the rest of the family waited.

Mrs. Canicula held out a cup of the black tea.

Lisa shook her head and held a hand up. "I'll be fine."

"You should have a little before we go," she said.

Lisa sighed and took the cup into the kitchen, pretended to take a sip, and then dumped the rest down the drain. This wasn't the way she wanted to start the day, but she did not want to deal with a sour stomach on top of the nerves already skittering under her skin.

She turned back to the family waiting in the doorway, pasted a smile on her face, and followed them to the church in the center of town.

The somber mood even bled out into the sky, pulling the clouds overhead and blocking the sun from shining down on the valley. It made for an even more heart-wrenching display. The closed coffin looked like an ominous premonition, and Lisa slumped in the seat, trying to disappear from the eyes of the congregation as they sought her out for reassurances she could not give.

Even the widow's gaze found hers when she stood next to the casket. Her eyes pleaded in a way that moved Lisa's soul.

She would not let this happen to another citizen of Opal.

As soon as the funeral was over, Lisa bowed out before she could get cornered at the reception. She made her way back to the house and closed herself in her bedroom to pack a sack for later that evening. Going out into the deep woods at night was not the smartest thing she thought to do, but it was necessary so she wouldn't have to worry about Herk or anyone else who decided to take up arms with her against the killing beast.

The soft knock on her door jerked her around, and she slid the backpack under her bed before she crossed and opened the door. Herk gripped both sides of the doorjamb and stared at the floor. The muscles in his arms bulged under the tight dress shirt covering them.

When he finally raised his gaze to her, she shivered at the resolve in his eyes.

He didn't speak. Instead, he moved into the room and kicked the door closed as he grabbed her arms and pinned her against the wall. Before her brain caught up to his actions, his lips were on hers.

Her eyes widened and she tried to shove him away but only succeeded in trapping her arms between them when he pressed his weight against her. She jerked her knee up, right into his family jewels. His grip on her dropped as he groaned and fell to his knees, gripping his balls.

"Don't you ever do that again," Lisa seethed and scooted away, putting distance between them before she decided to dropkick him.

He put his head on his arm and stayed that way for so long that Lisa took a tentative step forward. He put his hand out to stop her.

"I'm fine, just..." he said with a voice tight with pain. "I thought..." He wiped his face and looked up at her.

"You thought if you kissed me, it would change my mind?"

His old half smile that made him more than endearing appeared, and he shrugged.

She took a seat on the edge of her bed. "Herk, I've never seen you as anything other than an overprotective big brother." She finally voiced the silent narrative ranting in her head. "You're my oldest friend. You and Molly down the way were the only ones in this town who seemed to accept me when I arrived." She looked down at her hands. She hadn't seen Molly since Herk started his insane magic training sessions. "I think the last couple of years has clouded that enough to sour me even on a friendship with you. What we have is not healthy the way it once may have been. It's more of a rivalry to you. You proposing just seemed... wrong."

"And you could never see beyond friendship?" Hurt flared in his eyes and bled into his voice.

She shook her head. She did not want to give him false hope. Better to squash it now than to lead him on and have to do it later. "No." She refrained from expanding on the age differences or pointing out his unflattering obsessions.

His gaze hardened, and he gave her a nod like he was somehow coming to terms with her words. "You're going to be twenty-one next week," he said as if that was the end of the world.

In Opal it might have been. By twenty-one, most maidens were married. But Lisa wasn't most maidens. In the years when she should have been dating, Herk had her trying to start a fire where there wasn't any. It had been like asking her to get blood from a stone, and if that was his idea of courting a woman, god help the girl he finally settled down with.

"And?" she asked, even though she knew it was a loaded question that he would happily shoot at.

"You have no other prospects," he said and stood tall, crossing his arms. His face still held some of the redness from when she had kneed him, but the blotchy spots were probably more from anger than physical pain.

"So what? I'm supposed to get all aflutter at your magnanimous pity proposal? Just get out." She pointed at the door.

He took a step towards her, and she stood, shifting into a fighting stance. He smiled at her and an utterly inappropriate, mischievous light flared in his eyes. They narrowed as if she had become his prey.

"What the hell is wrong with you?"

"I like it when you get all feisty," he purred in a way that shot fear through her. "Besides, if you're going to go after the tiger on your own, don't you want to know what it feels like to be with a man before you die?"

She clenched her fists tighter as he took another step closer. "Get out."

"That is something I can successfully teach you," he said and reached for his belt buckle.

"I swear if you come any closer, the next shot I get in will break something down there permanently." She looked at his crotch and then back at his face pointedly. "And if that doesn't work, I'll claw your eyes out," she added when he continued to pull his belt from the loops.

The sound of the front door closing downstairs paused Herk's progress. It also seemed to clear the darkness from his features. He glanced over his shoulder and then back at Lisa. He pointed at her and then turned, storming out of the room before his mother or father came upstairs.

Lisa sagged back onto her bed on shaking legs. If they hadn't come home when they did, she wasn't sure what Herk would have done. Something had snapped in his mind, because her oldest friend would have never gone on attack mode like that. He would have protected her to the death.

She had to leave as soon as the opportunity presented itself. Otherwise, she was leaving herself vulnerable.

Chapter 6

"LISA?" MRS. CANICULA'S WORRIED voice came through the wooden door. "You didn't come for dinner when I called," she added, and then the door swung open. Mrs. Canicula smiled as she carried a tray into the room with a steaming bowl of stew and sliced bread.

"I wasn't hungry," Lisa said and straightened, but her stomach betrayed her, rumbling at the delicious scent coming from the dinner.

"Sounds like you are now." She smiled and set the tray at the foot of the bed. "Are you and Herk fighting?"

Lisa didn't quite know what to say to Herk's mother. If she said yes, the woman was sure to pry into why they were fighting, and she didn't want to tell her that her son was becoming a monster.

"He's been harder on me the last few weeks," she said, leaving it at that.

"Well, he's just trying to protect you." She turned to leave and pointed at the tray. "I'll be back in a little while to grab that when you are done."

She dug into the food and finished it faster than she had eaten in a while. She wished she had been downstairs for dinner and could've had seconds, but she could not face Herk after his earlier near assault.

She picked up the teacup and walked to the bathroom, dumped the tea down the drain, and then replaced it on the tray. That was the only benefit of eating in her room. There was no oversight, and she did not have to choke down the tea. Maybe she would do this more often when she got back from her mission. It sure beat hurting Mrs. Canicula's feelings.

Lisa brought the tray downstairs and put it in the sink while Mrs. Canicula was preoccupied with the laundry in the backyard. On the return trip to her room, she grabbed her winter coat and boots and stowed them under her bed along with her backpack and duffel with a warm waterproof sleeping bag.

As soon as both Mr. and Mrs. Canicula went to bed, she was leaving this house. She would brave the bitter winter wind over waking up with Herk climbing on top of her in her sleep. If he was out drinking, that was apt to be the end result when he got home. She had more of a chance surviving the white tiger.

She remained awake until the whispered good nights came through her door. When the hall lights extinguished, Lisa went into action. She pulled on her warmest pants and laced up her boots. She tucked in her thermal nightshirt and pulled on a thick sweater before slipping on her jacket and gloves. The heavy scarf easily wrapped around her head and neck before she pulled up her hood.

Lisa bound the duffel bag to her backpack and then put it on, clipping it and securing it tight. She moved as silently as possible to the door and gripped the knob.

Her heart jumped into her throat at the sound of the front door below, and the stumbling that followed had her shuffling to the window. She had climbed out it once on a dare from Herk and nearly broke her leg. But she hadn't been as tall as she was now. She'd have to toss the backpack out of range before she jumped out. Otherwise, she *would* break her leg.

Rushing, she pushed the window open, unclipped the backpack, and heaved it out the window. It sailed far enough away to not impede her drop from the sill once she got outside.

Herk's footsteps reached the stairs, and she could hear him murmuring but didn't wait to find out what he was saying.

Her heart drummed in her chest, and she threw her leg out of the window and turned, sliding her other leg out as she gripped the sill with her gloved hands. The moment she slid out the window, her door opened. She didn't wait. She lowered herself to her full length and let go.

Herk's hand slammed down on hers, pinning her in place. He glared down at her from her window. "Where do you think you're going?" he asked with breath that stank like a brewery.

Lisa tried to wiggle her hand free as he reached out with his other hand. She swatted it away and curled her fingers so his grip would slide off her glove. Just like that, the fabric slipped off her hand, and she was freefalling to the ground.

Herk's face disappeared from the window, and then she hit the ground, stumbling back onto her ass. She stood on shaking legs and grabbed her backpack in an all-out run towards the woods. If Herk caught her, she knew what he would do. She saw enough in his drunken eyes.

His lumbering footsteps crunched the snow behind her.

"If I catch you, you will regret saying no to me!" His growling voice echoed off the snow.

A yank on her backpack jerked her, and she glanced back at Herk. He had a strap in his hand and an insane smile like he had just caught the brass ring at the fair.

She let go of the pack and put everything she had into running as fast as she could. She was sure it wasn't just her virtue on the line. If he caught her, that was not the only thing he would do to her.

She didn't stop once she breached the forest. She dodged the tree branches and hurdled over the low bushes. Her heart thundered in her chest and her breath wheezed.

Still, he came after her, sounding like a wrecking ball taking on the forest. She darted to her right and slid beneath a prickly thistle bush. Covering her mouth, she forced herself to breathe as shallowly as she could.

Herk barreled by her, but his pace slowed down to a stop a few hundred feet away, illuminated by a patch of moonlight. He circled around looking at the pristine snow surrounding him.

A bitter wind rustled through the trees, blowing the snow around and covering her slide under the bush. It was almost as if the gods didn't want Herk to find her either.

"I will hunt you down, Lisa," he shouted. "And when I do, I am not taking no for an answer. Do you understand me?"

She shivered but remained silent as he stomped his way back to the edge of the woods.

"And if the white tiger gets you, I will not mourn your loss," he added.

The crunching snow became more distant with every step away from the woods. It wasn't until she heard the door slam that she let out a breath and crawled out from under the bush.

She had nothing. No sleeping sack. No clothes beyond what was on her back, and no weapons. And she couldn't go back to the house to try to retrieve her bow from the shed like she had planned to do before she snuck away.

She was on her own, weaponless, and her pocket wasn't going to keep her ungloved hand warm enough in the whipping wind. She stood on shaking legs and headed away from the house. It was the only direction where she had a slim chance of surviving the night unscathed.

Chapter 7

THE NIGHT BLANKETED LISA in heavy doubt. She had used Herk's footprints to the clearing, but she knew his tracking skills. No matter how much the wind blew, she knew he would eventually find her. She just hoped she wouldn't run into a bear or a pack of wolves in the meantime.

She dragged a tree branch she found behind her to try to obscure her footprints, which was fine in the woods, but now that she was in an open meadow, there was no hiding the path she took.

That itch between her shoulders started in again, and she spun, scanning the woods for the owner. She prayed it wasn't Herk because she didn't have the strength or speed, even with the head start, to reach the other side of the tundra to make it to the safety of the woods.

Nothing but the wind.

She took a deep breath and slowly let it out as she did one last sweep of the woods behind her. When nothing out of the ordinary happened, she turned back to her destination.

Trudging through the heavy snow slowed her down, and when she finally made it to the woods, she glanced back towards town. The path she'd crossed was no longer visible. She glanced at the branch. It had served her well covering her tracks, and it might provide her some sticks if she could find a rock to shave the ends. Her survival depended on her having something to defend herself with.

It might not be against the wildlife either.

She needed to reach the catacombs of shallow caves and find one to protect her from the unrelenting wind. Her entire body ached, and she needed to hunker down and get some rest before sunrise came.

She let the woods swallow her. The snow thinned here because the canopy was so thick, and not even the moon penetrated. She slowed and closed her eyes to try to let them adjust. If it weren't for the snow blown in from the tundra reflecting some ambient light, she wouldn't even be able to see the trees.

She picked up her pace, trying to recall the route through the trees. The only sound was the crunch of her boots and the brush dragging behind her. She prayed it was enough to keep the predators away.

Just as she reached the clearing with the caves in sight, rustling behind her stopped her in her tracks. She slowly turned, changing the grip on the tree branch to bring it up like a stickball bat at her shoulder. As silently as possible, she backed away from the woods under the bright light of the full moon. Each crunch of snow was as loud as a branch snapping and she cringed.

Above her frantic heartbeat drumming in her ears, she heard low growls. Whatever was on the hunt was not a single beast. If she ran, she would be brought down like a wild antelope. She continued her retreat, and after a dozen steps, eyes peered out from the dark forest. She gripped the branch tighter and gulped down her fear.

"Well, don't just hide in the woods. If you're going to attack, attack," she snarled and checked her footing to make sure she would get a full sweep with her makeshift weapon.

The lead wolf stepped out from the shadows with his lips drawn back from his deadly canines. Then a half dozen more fanned out on either side of the alpha, all snarling just as harshly.

If they attacked as one, she was doomed. Her chest tightened, and she dared to take a step back, and then another, and another. With each step, she reset her grip on the branch. They advanced at an equal pace, fanning out even more.

She knew the drill. She had seen wolves take down a moose before. These bastards were trying to get behind her, and then they would attack.

Out of the corner of her eye, she saw something move. She swung towards it, but nothing was there. She swung the branch wide as she turned back to face the wolves, and they jumped back.

A ball of heat formed in the pit of her stomach, and her breath quickened. The wolf to her left launched, and she swung the branch again, giving it everything she had. The crack of wood against bone filled the air, followed by a sharp yelp. The branch snapped in half, leaving her with a piece that was shorter than her arm, making her even more vulnerable to their attack.

It was as if the pack sensed her mounting fear. Another wolf rushed forward. When she swung, it grabbed the end of the broken branch between its teeth and yanked it right out of her grip. Now she was defenseless against the pack.

She backed away and splayed her hands in front of her. "Easy now," she said, trying to keep the tremble out of her voice. Her heartbeat ran wild.

That shadow in the corner of her eye crept close enough that she couldn't ignore it. She pulled her gaze away from the wolves and froze in place at the sight before her. A beautiful and terrifying white tiger approached on silent paws, but his gaze was not on her. It was focused on the wolves.

She looked back in time to see the alpha launch at her.

Light, hot and deadly, flared from both her palms, blinding her. The magic she did not believe she possessed shot forth like a flame thrower, turning the wolf to dust before he reached her. It blasted from her as if she were a human bomb, depleting every drop of energy she had.

When the light faded, a wave of dizziness took hold. She took an unsteady step, trying to blink away the white spots dotting her vision.

“Damn,” she whispered, and then darkness
fell over her with the force of a falling anvil.

Chapter 8

LISA WOKE WITH A start, disoriented by the gray walls and the small fire burning near her. But it was the skinned squirrel slowly roasting over the flames that made her sit up straight. Another wave of dizziness hit, and she nearly collapsed again.

A soft chuff came from her right. She jolted, spinning around to an entry of a cave. Lying in the snow like a sentinel guarding her was the famed white tiger. His blue eyes remained locked on hers for a moment before he looked back out at the dawn-streaked sky.

She did not understand how she got here, or even how she'd started a fire and obtained a meal with no weapons, never mind skinned and impaled it on a stick.

She huffed. The tiger obviously wasn't capable of doing these things. Lisa looked around for any indication someone else had been here. Footprints. Clothing. Anything. But there were no signs of her benevolent savior.

She glanced between the fire and the sentry, unnerved. This was the beast attacking her town. Targeting the weak. She shook her head, bothered by the dichotomy of that versus the silent sentry posted at the entrance. Such a heinous beast surely would have killed her when she was unconscious. But instead, he was... protecting her?

He glanced back at her, his blue eyes shining bright in the low light. It was almost as if his eyes were human. They held kindness. Those were not the eyes of a killer.

Troubled, she focused on the food. Delicately, she removed the cooked squirrel and waited until it cooled enough to peel a piece off. The meat inside was tender and juicy, and after her first tentative bite, she devoured the entire thing until there were only bones and sinew left. She tossed it all in the fire and leaned back against the wall.

She stared at her hands. Had she produced magic? Or had it been a trick of her imagination?

The tiger chuffed as if she had spoken aloud, but he did not look her way. His ears twitched at something outside, and he stood facing the morning light letting it bathe his beautifully fierce face. His fur reflected oranges and pinks as the sun rose into the day. When he stretched, his lithe form stirred something deep inside Lisa.

It was as if the wild beast was speaking to her soul. The language was unfamiliar though. Still, the warmth inside her had nothing to do with the embers of the fire. It was as foreign to her as this predicament.

She climbed to her feet. Her legs shook, and she wasn't sure if it was weakness or nerves. Normally, she would run in the opposite direction of danger, but she couldn't help the draw pulling her toward the tiger.

He stood from his stretch and turned his head towards her, following her as she approached but he showed no signs of aggression. When she stepped beside him, she looked out over the valley. Her gaze drew to the woods, and she gasped at the blackened landscape. A half-moon of devastation had imprinted on the land. Even the snow hadn't blown over it. It was as if the blast had killed the wind.

"Did I do that?" she asked.

The tiger nodded his head as he chuffed at her.

"Holy…" Her legs gave out, and she fell to her knees, woozy. She held her hands out and stared at them. "I've never…" She couldn't think clearly enough to form a coherent sentence.

As much as she hated to admit it, Herk had been right, although it took a near-death experience to unlock the magic. She wiped her face, still staring at the blackened land.

"And you saved me from the wolves?"

The tiger shook his head. Very slowly. When his gaze fell on her she shivered at the hardness reflected in the blue of his eyes. He looked back at the scar on the land and poked his chin out before his gaze returned to hers. He stretched out on the ground next to her, his regal head held high as if he knew she was in awe of him.

She reached out and touched his silky fur. Just the connection filled her with warmth and stole her breath. His eyes closed, and he chuffed softly, almost like a purr. Her duty to kill this beautiful creature did not sit well.

"Did you kill a villager down there?" She pointed towards Opal in the distance.

He shook his head and glanced at her. There was a horror lit in his eyes that didn't belong on a tiger's face. Deep down where that warmth lit her soul, she knew the tiger was telling the truth.

Which meant there was some other evil plaguing the town. Something so heinous that they blamed the filthy lore. Lies passed on from generation to generation fueled someone's homicidal tendencies.

Who would do such a thing?

She didn't have an answer, but she needed one, even if it meant having to deal with Herk again. But she would wait until the sun was high enough in the sky that the town was awake and active. Otherwise, she might end up locked somewhere as Herk's plaything.

"I need to go back," she said, even though that chilled the warmth right out of her bones.

He leaned his big tiger head into her and rubbed her with his jaw, nearly knocking her over.

She climbed to her feet, and he stood as well.

"You can't go. They'll kill you." She knew the townsfolk too well. If she walked into town with the white tiger by her side, they would shoot him on sight, and she didn't know what they would do to her.

At least this way, she could fight for him without putting either of them in danger.

"I will return. I promise," she said and gently patted the tiger.

She wanted to figure out what this draw was all about and why when the tiger had shown up, her magic flared as if the door holding it in place had been ripped off by a twister.

Chapter 9

THE TREK BACK TO Opal was uneventful in comparison to the night before. The tiger had followed her into the woods, but at the entry to the tundra, she pointed back towards the caves.

"Stay. Please. I do not want to be responsible for you getting hurt." She waited until he had slunk out of sight before she headed across the snow without worrying about covering her tracks like she had the night before. If Herk was waiting for her, there was nothing she could do except fight.

She stepped out of the woods a little south of where Herk's house was. The quiet hit her. Usually by the time the sun was this high, the town was busy with the noises of living. She bypassed the Caniculas' house and walked down the middle of the street.

It wasn't until she got to her friend Molly's house that the hushed whispers from the back reached her ears. The pattern of too many footprints pulled her along, and when she rounded the corner, a small crowd had gathered around another body. Her brain stalled at the bloody snow and the red-stained animal prints.

She gasped. "Molly," she whispered as she stared at the body of her friend.

Constable Jones turned towards her with his hat tipped farther back than normal. His jaw was tight and his eyes suspicious.

"When?" she asked, still unable to draw a complete breath. Her only friend left in this godforsaken town was dead. Slaughtered like an innocent lamb. She drew a painful inhale of frigid air and tried to plow through the confusion clouding her mind.

Could the tiger that protected her really have done this? Horror, loss, and building anguish crested inside her. It didn't help that Herk was eyeing her from across the yard, and she couldn't quite bring herself to make eye contact, either. She knew the moment she did, the stinging tears she was holding back would escape.

"She had gotten up to feed her animals before work and never came back in," Constable Jones said.

Molly worked the early shift. She always got there just as the sky was painted with the sunrise. If that were the case, Lisa's tiger couldn't have done it because he was keeping watch over her in the cave. She swallowed the bile lining her throat and looked closer at the kill site.

"You need to stop this tiger before he kills again," Herk said from the other side of the crowd.

"How do you know it was the tiger?" she asked, still looking at the snow all around them.

Herk, along with Constable Jones, pointed at the tracks surrounding Molly. They were clearly tiger tracks, but she hadn't seen a sign of paw prints leaving the town, never mind a path of blood that was sure to stain the snow for at least a few feet. But outside of the prints around the body, there was no visible sign of exit, not even in the trampled path she had come on.

"Where are the footprints coming in or going out?" She waved at the snow in the backyard. The only pawprints were around her dead friend. "Did the tiger drop from the sky and then fly away?" She dared to send a sideways glare at Herk.

Red bloomed in his cheeks. "Lisa wasn't at the house at all this morning, and her bed didn't look like she even slept in it."

Anger surfaced. How dare he try to pin this on her.

She crossed her arms. "First it was the tiger who did this? Now you're trying to pin this on me?"

"Where were you?" Constable Jones asked, which given his job, made sense since he was investigating the death, but the fact Herk had put that seed of doubt there irked her.

"I was out there in the woods trying to stay alive, no thanks to Herk." She waved at him, but she still had a thread of loyalty for their former friendship left. "You'll find my footprints across the tundra to the far woods and beyond if needed," she added when Constable Jones narrowed his eyes.

"Your backpack was in the yard," Herk said, and a crease appeared in his brow.

"Yeah, well you scared me, and I dropped it," she said, but didn't explain any further. She didn't want to tell Constable Jones she was actually running away from Herk. That wouldn't look good considering they all were standing around a dead body.

Herk cocked his head like he was trying to remember the prior night.

"I went to try to find the tiger," she said softly.

"Alone?" His eyes widened in horror.

She didn't know whether Herk was acting or not. If he was, he was doing one hell of a job.

She raised her eyebrows. "Yes. The town council made it clear I needed to fix this problem or die trying, or were you not listening to them yesterday?"

She did not want to tell them that she had released some kind of magic last night. She didn't want to give Herk the satisfaction of being right after what he had pulled.

Could she forgive him for his drunken ramblings?

She had shot down his proposal, so he could have just been acting out. She let out a huff and glanced at her dead friend, and the loss hit, misting her eyes with unshed tears. Her chin started to tremble, and she turned and trudged out of the backyard, hell-bent on figuring out who, or what, was killing members of her town.

A hand landed on her shoulder, and Lisa instinctively yanked away, spinning to look Herk in the eye.

"Don't touch me," she hissed and swiped at the wet heat streaking her cheeks.

He pulled his hand back quickly. "Sorry," he mumbled and looked at the ground. "I know she was your friend."

More tears covered her eyes, blurring her vision. She nodded. She only had a few friends in Opal, and it seemed she had lost both of her close ones in the last twenty-four hours.

"You don't remember last night, do you?" She sniffled and wiped her nose.

He bit his lower lip and shook his head. "I had a real bender." He kicked at the snow again. "I found your backpack this morning. And then I heard Molly's mother screaming..." He looked at the ground.

Lisa swore there were tears in his eyes, but he blinked them away just as fast as they came.

"I thought the worst." He met her gaze.

"Then why did you make that comment about me being gone last night to the constable?" She didn't buy his innocent act, at least not all of it. He did look a little green this morning, and she hoped his hangover was as hellish as he had made her night.

"Because I'm still mad that you said no to my proposal," he said. "But not mad enough for my heart not to hammer in my chest at the thought of you getting hurt." He shuffled in place and crossed his arms as if he were protecting his very soul from any more harm.

"You are a very mean drunk, Herk. I ran because of you." She stabbed a finger into his chest, unable to contain the anger any longer.

His eyes widened, his arms fell, and then sadness and shame washed over his face. "I didn't..."

"No, you didn't. I got away before you could do anything you could never take back, but I saw a side of you that I had never seen before. I've seen you drunk, but not like that. And I detest that person who threatened to take whatever the hell he wanted. You may be the son of the head of the town council, but you are not above the law." She forced her voice to stay hushed so the lawmen in the vicinity wouldn't hear her.

"So why didn't you tell the constable?" he grumbled and glanced towards Molly's backyard.

"Because you were once my dearest friend, and I still have some insane loyalty to you and your family." She glanced at the people still milling around Molly's and decided the conversation about the prior night was over. "The white tiger did not do that," she said and looked back at Herk. "I don't know what did, but I'm going to find out."

She marched towards the Caniculas' house to get her backpack. As she rounded the corner, she saw it sitting next to the door along with Mr. Canicula.

Mr. Canicula stood and glared down at her like he believed she was some sort of criminal.

She slowed to a stop at the foot of the stairs. "It isn't the tiger," she said, looking up at him trying to gauge his reaction. His lips were thinned like he was pissed at her even approaching the house.

His eyes narrowed. "I have half a mind to lock you up for Molly's death."

Her mouth dropped in stunned silence. How could he think she had killed her friend?

She glanced down the street and back at him in confusion. "I didn't kill Molly," she said. "I don't know who did."

"It was the tiger, and you damn well know it."

Something deep inside her warned her not to say more. Not to tell this man that she knew it wasn't the tiger because he had been protecting her in the caverns. She didn't understand the voice inside her, but she obeyed and snapped her jaw closed. She took another step and reached for her backpack.

He shook his head and pointed towards the mountains. "Do your duty, or reap the repercussions," he growled.

"I'm planning on it, but I'd like to figure out who is killing people here before I go." She stared up at him, blocking the door and her pack.

"If you stay, you are going to jail for the murders." He crossed his arms and clenched his jaw.

She didn't understand why he was doing this. People in town were being killed, and it wasn't from a fabled beast like he seemed to think. "But..."

A wicked smile appeared, one that she had never seen before and one that spawned a thousand alarms in her head. When he leaned forward, she stepped back, putting distance between them as her flight response started blaring.

"I can put you in jail for life." He tapped his lips and looked at the sky. "Actually, I could put you in front of a firing squad, and then my son would move on and settle down with someone more his style."

So it was about her refusal to marry his son. "You bastard," she said.

"I've been called that a time or two, but just so you don't think too badly of our family, my wife insisted you take this with you," he said and tossed her a thermos. "Now go. Kill the tiger like you were meant to, and then maybe I'll rethink my position."

She stared at the silver canister in her hand and debated. Stay and get put in jail for something she didn't do, or go back to find the white tiger and figure out what really happened, both in town as well as with her magic? The choice was easy.

"Can I at least have my backpack and bow?"

His smile turned even meaner if that was even possible. "No. And I'll give you to the count of three to get moving before I change my mind."

Lisa turned towards the woods with only the canister of black tea that she knew would make her sick. But it might serve in a pinch if she couldn't find food.

What she really needed was that warm fire and answers that she would not find within a jail cell in Opal.

Chapter 10

WITH HER FOOTPRINTS STILL trackable in the snow, she found her way back to the area outside of the woods. She thought this was where the wolves had attacked, but the blackened earth was gone. The snow drifts were large enough to make her doubt her location. The mountainside of caverns didn't help, either. There was no telling which of the shadows facing Opal had been the one she was in earlier.

Her arms dropped by her side as she stared.

"Can I help you?"

She jumped and spun towards the deep voice. Sparks danced across her fingertips, and she clenched her fists, shocked at the sudden appearance of magic. She stared at her hands, dumbfounded, and then jerked her attention to the man standing near her.

People in Opal thought Herk was all the rage, but this man made Herk look like the ugly stepsister. His jet-black hair reached his shoulders and had a natural curl that most women would die for. His strong jaw was dabbled with stubble that she was sure would be scratchy against her skin. She was ashamed to admit she wanted to find out for sure. Both his hair and unshaven face made his eyes stand out even more. She had never seen eyes that bright blue. They glimmered like a glacial stream or the sky at noon in the fall. Deep. Penetrating. Intoxicating.

She blinked and stepped back. She *had* seen eyes that specific shade of blue before. She had seen them this morning, but they weren't a man's eyes. They were the eyes of the white tiger. Her heart pounded and her stomach rumbled like she hadn't eaten in days. She licked her lips but couldn't stop staring.

"Can I help you?" he asked again, and a smile toyed with his lips, making him all the more devastatingly attractive.

She giggled and heat rose in her cheeks. His question finally knocked her out of her stupor, and she turned her gaze back to the wall of caves, silently cursing her lack of being able to get her brain and mouth to work together to articulate.

"I... uh... I was looking for the cave that I woke in this morning."

"I can help you if you'd like." He held his hand out to her. "My name's Elijah."

She stared at his outstretched hand for longer than customary, and when he started to pull it back, she grabbed it and shook like she had zero manners. She stared at the connection in shock as her entire body filled with magic, as if whatever had been keeping it dormant had finally burst free. *What the hell?*

It engulfed her, and she breathed deeply. The scents surrounding the two of them were wild, like a raging river, or the air right before a thunderstorm. With it came the undertones of his unique musky scent that put her hormones into overdrive. Along with thrilling her, his touch was also calming, like the cadence of the sea.

His smile faded and his eyes widened. "You are the fated one," he whispered and seemed to squeeze a fraction tighter as if he never wanted to let go.

Her moment of awe ended like a crack of thunder on a clear day. She yanked her hand away. "I am not killing the tiger," she snapped.

His smirk deepened. "I would hope not," he said with a chuckle. "Come on, let's find a fire and get you warmed up." He started walking towards the caves.

She hesitated. He was a stranger, after all.

He stopped a few steps away and glanced over his shoulder. He reached down and pulled a knife out of a sheath on his leg that she hadn't noticed, and her heart lurched.

This could be the killer!

He flipped the knife around and held the hilt out to her. "I promise I won't bite, but if you need something to feel more secure about following someone you don't know, here."

She stared at it and slowly took it from him, unsure of whether she felt safer or not with a weapon in her hand. In all of Herk's physical training, he had proven how easily someone could be relieved of their weapon. She narrowed her gaze.

There were no warning alarms going off inside her like there had been at the Caniculas', and she had to trust her instincts. They usually didn't lead her astray. She nodded. "Normally I don't follow strangers, but a warm fire does sound nice."

He smiled and she nearly melted in the snow with the effect it had on her. Warm and gushy like holding a baby for the first time, and she wanted to smack herself. This wasn't like her. She was more the cynical one and not the one to get mushy or drool over a man. Plus, the warm and wild connection she felt when they were shaking hands was something she couldn't ignore.

The path wound up the mountain passing by some of the lower indentations. When he stepped into the first real cavern, she hesitated at the sight of the smoldering fire. She thought she could make out bones in the ashes, but he threw a couple more logs on the embers, burying whatever she thought she saw.

He leaned over and blew on the fire to fan the flames to life, and her brain stalled when his gaze found hers. Just watching him stirred things inside Lisa that she had never experienced before. It was almost on the edge of euphoria, but that made no sense. She shook the thoughts out of her head and stepped inside near the fire as he settled back on his knees.

Lisa set the blade on the rock next to her, glancing around. "Is this... yours?" She waved at the place.

He nodded.

"So... you're the one who brought me here last night and cooked a squirrel for me?"

Color filled his cheeks, and he glanced at the fire with a small nod.

"Thank you," she said with a mouth that was suddenly so dry she considered Mrs. Canicula's tea. She wanted to ask about the tiger, but her tongue stuck to the roof of her mouth. She needed a drink and opened the thermos.

Elijah's head snapped up the moment she unscrewed the cap. He nearly jumped over the fire and grabbed the container from her. "You brought their poison here?" he bellowed.

Lisa's eyes went wide, and she scrambled for the knife, jumped to her feet, and pressed herself into the wall. Her knife hand shook just as much as the rest of her trembling body.

He dumped the contents in the fire, and instead of dousing the flame like the tea should have, it acted as an accelerant, turning the small fire into a blaze.

"Where did you get this?" He held the container out like it was as deadly as the flames licking the ceiling of the cave.

"Mr. Canicula," she said, steadying the knife in case he dared to get any closer. She had had enough of being the victim with Herk. She wasn't going to let a stranger get the best of her. "I know it's awful-tasting, but poison? Really?"

He gave her a deadly glare. "And you were going to try to give it to me?" he growled, and even in his anger, he was beautiful to behold, like an angry angel might be.

She nearly hissed at her inappropriate thoughts, growing just as irate as Elijah. "No. I was thirsty!" she yelled at him. "I was going to have a drink, and look what you did!" She pointed the knife at the blaze.

"You drink *this*?" He shook the container at her, acting more like Herk than the gentleman she met at the edge of the woods.

"Not by choice," she snapped. "But it is all I was given when I was driven out of Opal. So, sue me if I wanted a drink."

He recoiled with wide eyes and seemed to calm again. "You really drink this?" he asked, and a confused crease marred his perfect forehead.

She shrugged. "I was never fond of it, but the Caniculas have made me drink a cup every day since my parents died."

He slowly paled. "When was that?" he asked with a voice so full of trepidation that she almost laughed and would have if her heart wasn't pounding in her throat from the adrenaline rush.

"Since I was four."

"Jesus," he whispered and turned, pitching the thermos out the cave with a growl.

He paced the entry, mumbling under his breath. It looked like he was having an argument with himself. Every time he stole a glance in her direction, she gripped the knife tighter. She didn't know what to think of him, and if she had a different place to hunker down, she would have been gone in a heartbeat.

He finally stopped and stared towards Opal. His shoulders dropped as if the wind had whispered a calming truth. When he turned, he was wearing the mask of the kind man she'd met at the edge of the woods.

"You said something when I called you the fated one." He approached the fire again. "Why would the fated one kill the white tiger?" he asked with genuine curiosity.

"Haven't you heard the fable about the white tiger?"

He nodded. "That's why I'm asking. I don't understand."

She cocked her head. "That's the lore," she said as if he were shy a few marbles. "The white tiger wakes and slaughters the innocent. He wants to destroy Opal, and only the fated one's magic can kill the tiger and stop the reign of terror."

With each word, his eyes saddened until a tear slipped from the corner of his eye, and all she felt was his despair.

He slowly sank to his knees facing her. "No, child. That is not the true prophecy." He wiped his face and stared up at her. "You've been fed poison in more than one way."

"What do you mean poison?" She lowered the knife but wasn't ready to sit back down and leave herself vulnerable.

The fire still blazed sending white and red embers like rain.

"Tea steeped with tar." He waved at the fire to make his point. "Did anyone else in the house drink it?"

Lisa went to nod, but tilted her head trying to remember Herk drinking his mother's tea. Herk's parents drank wine or water and rarely had a teacup in front of their seats at dinner. Now that Elijah mentioned it, she was sure she had been the only one that drank Mrs. Canicula's tea.

Finally, she shook her head. "But why would they poison me?" she whispered and continued to stare at the fire.

"Tea steeped with tar is a magical eliminator. It kills magic and then kills the host." His lips pressed tightly together. "By all standards, you should have died before your fifth birthday."

"Bullshit," she said and reset her grip on the knife. She shifted away from him. She didn't know this man, and the suggestions he was making made her skin itch with unease.

"The true prophecy, the one that was written in the history books by scholars of long ago, stated that when the white tiger woke from a long winter's sleep, he would unite with the fated one to rid Opal of all forms of evil and bring true peace to the region." He bit his lower lip and looked at the ceiling. "But it seems the monsters who initially bound the tiger in frost have been very, very busy." His voice turned feral, and he pressed his lips together shaking his head. Elijah climbed to his feet and glared at her. "Tell me everything."

"Why should I tell you anything?"

He stared into her eyes with an intensity that made her take a step away from him. "Because I am the white tiger, and the people who imprisoned me were named Canicula."

"How is that even possible?" she spit out.

He stared at her but didn't say a word.

Lisa leaned back and laughed. He was talking gibberish. That would mean he was hundreds of years old and he really was some type of strange monster that looked like a twenty-five-year-old man. That was just not possible.

"Right. And I'm the Queen of Sheba."

"Proof it is." He closed his eyes, and the wind picked up, sending a funnel into the small cavern, spraying smoke everywhere. A fresh breeze cleared the smoke, and the white tiger stood right where Elijah had been. The tiger cocked his head and raised a single brow, challenging her.

She stumbled back and fell on her ass. The knife clattered on the rock next to her. Her wide eyes matched the shock pounding her heart in staccato beats.

Her mind stalled at the implications. "But... how?"

The wind blasted through the opening again, and she squinted trying to blink through the blinding smoke. This time when it cleared, Elijah stood tall and crossed his arms. His eyebrow remained cocked the way it had as a tiger.

"I am a tiger shifter." He shrugged. "The Caniculas were my people's natural enemy. I am the last one of my kind thanks to those vampires. They thrive on chaos and fear, and when desperate, they will drink the blood of the innocent. They are the true evil haunting Opal."

She laughed again and picked up the knife to give her some edge against Elijah if she needed it.

She could not see the Caniculas in the same light that Elijah was painting them. Herk's father was an asshole, so maybe he could be some long lost relative of those he was describing, but vampire? Come on. They didn't even have pointy teeth.

"If you had told me they were power hungry bastards, I would have believed you, but monsters, like out of a fiction book?" She shook her head.

He licked his lips. "Randolph Canicula?" he asked, and her smirk faded. "And his lovely wife Serinya whose hair looks as smooth as ancient Egyptian hair plates? Not a usual name these days, I'm sure, but it was fairly popular when she was created."

She narrowed her gaze. "You could have heard their names in Opal or seen her on the street." She was beginning to doubt this man had any honorable intentions like she'd originally thought. "They practically raised me after my parents died, so why should I take the word of something that is supposed to be evil? That's supposed to have killed people in my town. My home. Give me one good reason why I should stay here. Why should I not do my duty and kill you?" She pointed the blade at him.

"Because I have not breached the barrier since I woke three years ago." He pointed towards Opal. "And I have every reason to. Randolph Canicula burned my fated mate at the stake at what they call the great fire circle just before he dragged me to the mountains and bound me in ice for three hundred years. But I didn't because revenge is not justice." He sent a glare at her and wiped his mouth. "And because deep down you know that tea was poison." He pointed at her.

As much as she didn't want to admit it, in the very essence of her soul she knew he was telling her the truth. And with Mr. Canicula's reaction to her today, she conceded that Elijah was more trustworthy than either of the men who had lived under the same roof with her since she was four.

"Have you ever killed before?" she snapped, still gripping the knife like it was her last hope.

"I've killed to eat."

She recoiled.

He rolled his eyes. "Squirrels, pigs, deer, all manner of beasts."

Her eyes narrowed, and mistrust laced her mouth with bitterness. "Define all manner of beasts."

"Bears, wolves, other large cats. But your real question is, have I killed people?"

She nodded.

"I have never killed a human being, and I do not intend to start now." He took a seat on the opposite side of the fire and waved for her to sit.

Deep down in her soul, she recognized the truth.

"Then who is killing the townspeople of Opal?" she asked and lowered the knife. She took a seat on the ground and put the blade down to show she was willing to trust him, but it was close enough to leave the alliance uneasy.

He shrugged and reached behind the nearest rock. She tensed until she saw a canteen in his hand along with some dried jerky.

"You said you were thirsty," he said and offered her the canteen and half the food.

She took it and tested a small sip from his canteen. Cool, crisp water washed over her tongue, and she took a longer pull of the refreshing drink. It flowed down her tight throat, easing the dryness of the fire-heated cave. She put the jerky aside, not ready to eat just yet. Her stomach was in too many knots.

"So, what's your story?" He took a bite of the jerky, and just the action of his lips pressing against the dried meat sidetracked her for a moment.

She shook the thoughts away and focused on his blue eyes, but that was no better. "What do you want to know?" she asked, trying to focus on anything else but the shifter across the fire.

"Let's start with your name." He smiled, and it completely disarmed her.

"My name is Lisa. Lisa Winters."

"Lisa, please start at the very beginning," he said in a soft voice that almost lulled her into trusting him.

She took another sip from the canteen and handed it back, avoiding the food he had offered. Her stomach was nervous enough, so food would just turn it into a roiling mess, especially if she was going to start at the beginning of her own short tragedy.

Chapter 11

WITH A DEEP BREATH and an internal pep talk, she glanced at the cave's opening. A snow squall had just started, wiping out the vision of Opal in the distance. The snow didn't reach where they were. Neither did the howling wind, but it provided the perfect backdrop for her to start her sad story.

"I wasn't born in Opal. I was born in the lowlands where it never snowed. I still remember the vast green fields and the even greener trees lining the winding river that our house was on.

It was just as stunning a view as Opal's white opulence." She traced her finger on the rock floor, taking in the natural chill radiating from the surface. "I was four when the floods came. Our house was destroyed when the river rose, and we were left with nothing but the clothes on our backs." She wrapped her arms around herself and shivered.

Elijah threw a few more logs onto the fire. The blaze devoured the wood, warming the rock and her surroundings.

"My father decided it was time for us to see his home." She smiled. "I was amazed by the mountains and all the white blanketing the land." She closed her eyes. "Did you know snow has a scent?"

"Yes."

His soft answer opened her eyes, and the wistful look on his face made her want to cross over and wrap her arms around him until he smiled again. Instead, she dropped her gaze to the flames and continued.

"Newly fallen snow has the same smell as a freshly cleaned baby, and I can remember stepping out of the carriage and inhaling. That was the first taste of Opal I truly had. And it was glorious until the scrumptious smells of the bakeries mingled with the scent of the snow. It was a lot for my four-year-old self to take in all at once. I had wanted to cherish each one separately, but they layered together, cheapening the experience."

She let out a small chuckle at the memory of that first day. Lisa had been awed by Opal. She could still feel the tingle that traveled her spine as she took in the town center.

"By the time we got to the town center, I was so in awe of the place that I stopped walking and just stared up at the grandeur of the town hall. I had never seen something so tall." She sighed. "My parents were in a hurry to get to the house we were staying at, but I didn't want to leave that spot. It was as if the place called to me. When they tried to move me along, I don't know what came over me. Maybe I was tired from the trip or had sensory overload, but I jumped right into tantrum mode and my fingers started shooting sparks, like mini strips of gun powder being lit. The sensation overwhelmed me." She glanced at Elijah. "That was the last time I had the ability to tap into magic until last night."

"I'm surprised you were able to produce any at all," he said and took another bite of food. He nodded to her pile, but she shook her head and offered them to him. "You should eat a little," he said and pushed her hand back.

She broke off a small piece and chewed on the end. "I don't know how I did it. I've been drilled in so many failed training sessions since I turned eighteen and not a flicker."

"The tea should have made it impossible."

Lisa bit into the jerky, taking a bigger piece of the salty hide to make the memory of the black sludge on her tongue go away. "I should have known," she said and looked at him. "That stuff, it was gross. And Mrs. Canicula kept telling me it would help me find my magic." She shuddered.

"What happened at the town hall?" he asked, pulling her back to the conversation.

Lisa appreciated the redirection. "Nothing really. Just a few murmured whispers before my parents whisked me away to our new home. It was much sparser than the house on the river. But then again, we didn't have much left, and Opal was the only place we had relatives."

"So, you had family here?" He leaned forward.

"Had being the operative word. By the time we arrived, my grandmother was on her death bed. My parents wouldn't let me go into the sick room for fear I might catch whatever it was that was wasting my grandmother away. I only saw a glimpse of her through the cracked door, and she looked like a skeleton with a human skin stretched over it. It gave me nightmares for years, and I've seen that same affliction a couple of times since my grandmother died. It was as if their life was being slowly drained from their bones, and there was nothing they could do to stop it."

Elijah nodded as she talked, like there wasn't anything said that he didn't expect or see in his lifetime either.

"Grandma passed away within days of our arrival. I met Herk at the funeral, and he was such a fun boy. He wanted to know if I wanted to come to his birthday party in a few days. There was a nine-year difference between us, but he talked with me for a very long time. Looking back, it seems a bit strange." She bit her lip and wondered why he hadn't gone to play with the kids his age instead of sitting and talking to the lonely new girl. She shook the thoughts away. "Well, my mother thought that was a wonderful idea, but my father was skeptical. When Herk said the party was just for kids, my father gave me permission to go."

She smiled. "I remember my mother sewing a beautiful party dress for me, and she did my hair nicely before both my parents walked me to the party. I thought the town hall was the big thing. Well, Herk Canicula's birthday parties were spectacular, especially for a four-year-old who'd never had more than a cupcake and my parents singing 'Happy Birthday.' I didn't know where to look. Bright, shiny balloons hung from posts leading guests to the actual party spot."

Lisa's smile faded as the memory came barreling back in full color in her mind. The bittersweet memory shed tears from her eyes. "I didn't even say goodbye to my parents. I just ran towards the colorful chaos."

She met Elijah's gaze, and he handed her the canteen. She was grateful and sucked down a mouthful of water, letting the coolness coat her mouth before she returned it to him. She wiped her face, erasing the tears that had formed.

"I wish I had hugged them goodbye. If I had known I would never see them again..." She looked out at the swirling snow and pressed her knuckle to her lips.

Elijah moved closer and took her hand. The calmness of his touch gave her control again, and she squeezed his hand before releasing it.

"Thank you," she said, cleared her throat, and stripped her jacket, laying it over the rock next to her. "My parents were late in picking me up, and Mrs. Canicula brought me into the kitchen and handed me a cup of her black tea. She waited until I choked it down before telling me that my parents had died."

She picked at a hangnail on her thumb while Elijah waited for her to continue. Her mind shot off like a rocket exploding in a million different directions as she started scrutinizing her memories.

A slow burn started in the pit of her stomach, making her feel sick. All the hidden things she should have seen were starting to swirl in her head, and she climbed to her feet. Pacing helped and then horrible truths started revealing themselves until the tingling of sparks on her fingertips drew her out of her own reverie.

"They poisoned me every day since I was four." The verbal confirmation sent her heart into overdrive as her fingers ignited and flames warmed her skin.

Elijah sat unaffected by her display. It was as if he had known these things but needed her to figure them out on her own.

He raised an eyebrow and nodded. "For someone who has been fed poison for sixteen years, you most certainly have a huge untapped reservoir of power," he said and hopped to his feet.

She stared through him as a new horrifying thought surfaced. "They killed my parents?" she asked and then focused on his blue eyes. "And fed me lie after lie about you?" Her voice rose higher.

He put his hand on her arm in an attempt to calm her. The connection doused the fire sparking from her hands, but it did nothing to stave off the building fury inside her.

"Why would they lie? Why would they..." She paused, and her eyes widened. "Would they kill the people of their own town?" She searched his kind eyes.

"Caniculas are evil creatures escaped from the bowels of hell. Those skeletons with skin stretched over them are the victims of Canicula greed. The fact they bore an offspring while I slept is even more concerning," he said and glanced out towards the town. "If they are the same soulless bastards they were back when I walked this earth the first time, then I wouldn't put it past them to kill members of the community in an effort to frame me." He met her gaze. "Especially since they had to have known I was awake, or at the very least waking soon."

"How did they know that?" She scoffed, still uneasy with the idea of them being actual monsters.

He pointed at her. "You. You're turning twenty-one next week if I'm not mistaken."

She took a step away from him and nodded, expecting the type of pep-talk that Herk delivered the other night.

"If they truly believed you were the fated one, they know the fable and would do anything to stop the prophecy from coming true. They knew the white tiger would claim you on your twenty-first birthday."

"Wait. What?" She took another step back. Her mind spun with doubt. Doubt for which fable was truth. Doubt for everything she had been taught, for every conversation. For every single lie she was fed. All because a handsome stranger was feeding her a line.

"What the hell do you mean by claim me?" She glanced across the space at the knife where she had been sitting kicking herself for not grabbing it before she had her mini rant. "I am not claimable," she snapped and set herself in a fight stance.

He let out a soft laugh and moved back to his seat by the fire. "I guess men don't claim women anymore?" Elijah shrugged and leaned against the wall. "But that's not an option. They've made that impossible now."

Her stomach dropped to the ground at the disappointment raking her skin. Just a moment ago, the thought of being claimed rubbed her into a frenzy and now that he'd proclaimed it was impossible, she was disturbed? *Make up your mind, girl.*

Confusion shadowed her thoughts, and she stepped farther away from him. "Why is it impossible?" she asked, and she despised the pout in her voice.

"They poisoned you. Hence any union would poison me in a way you do not want to witness." He kicked at the dirt. "Theoretically speaking."

"What the hell does that mean?"

"It means that maybe you're not toxic, but I'm not willing to find out, especially since you seem so dead set against the idea."

When she didn't dignify him with a comment, he continued, "Theoretically, you should not have been able to produce an ounce of magic. Yet you did." He waved at her like presenting a gift.

She stared down at her hands and cocked her head. If she had been poisoned with a serum that was supposed to kill off her magic, why didn't it work? Was the white tiger the one who was lying to her?

She crossed to the opening of the cave and swept her gaze over the forest below. Elijah had been nothing but a gentleman to her. If he wanted to claim her as callously as Herk had wanted to, she wouldn't have been clothed and cared for this morning. He had ample time and opportunity to take advantage of her. But he hadn't.

Besides, he wasn't lying about killing her friend. The timing of Molly's death just so happened to coincide with his display of kindness.

However, the thought of the Caniculas being evil didn't mesh with the fact they'd taken her in and given her a home. They provided food and clothing and a roof over her head. They provided her with a lifelong friend in their son.

And yet, Mr. Canicula had sent her to what he thought was certain death. Why?

"What happens if you are killed?" she asked with her back to him.

Elijah remained quiet and she turned around.

"Their evil will spread outside of Opal. Deaths will increase tenfold from what you saw in Opal. They've been cautious because of the small community, but that will end if the boundary is destroyed. I'm the only thing keeping them bound to this location."

"And if I die?"

His lips formed a grimace. "Then if the lore is true, I would die, too. I'm as bound to the fated one as they are bound to this town."

Lisa reached for the wall. "And what if I was to marry a Canicula?" she asked in a hushed whisper, meeting his gaze.

His rosy cheeks paled, and his eyes widened in true horror. He shook his head. "The Caniculas would inherit your magic, and all would truly be lost."

Lisa's knees weakened and she dropped to the ground. She knew Herk's ambitions. She knew his obsession with her magic. And she glimpsed the monstrous side of him the other night. Could he truly be that manipulative?

"I am such a fool."

Hands landed on her shoulders. "Tell me you aren't married to one of them," he said with a strained voice that matched his tight grip.

"No. But their son *did* ask me to marry him. He said he wanted an alliance. A partnership to defeat the white tiger," she said and let out a high-pitched laugh.

"And you said?"

"I said no. He's too much like an older brother to me. Everything about it was all wrong."

Elijah's face relaxed.

"But it all makes sense now. The tea, the relentless failed magic training day after day. And then the recent deaths made to look like tiger attacks, and the final straw was Mr. Canicula's sending me out here to basically die."

"Either way, it suits their purpose," he said. "If you are the fated one, your death would kill both of us. If you aren't, then it is the perfect way to get rid of you."

Her stomach rolled, but she swallowed the bitter bile. Good God. Every scenario, every facet

of her life to this moment had all been a grand
manipulation in the pursuit of Canicula power.

Chapter 12

"I HAVE TO GO back to Opal," Lisa said as she grabbed her coat and slipped it on. She headed towards the opening.

Elijah scrambled off the floor and stepped in front of her. "You should try to harness your magic a little before you step into a hostile situation." He put his hands out, splaying his fingers in an effort to stop her. "Please."

"What if they kill again? Do you want that on your head?" She finished buttoning her coat and glared up at him.

Elijah closed his eyes. "Think about what you're doing."

"I am." She went to step out of the cave.

"I can't let you go," he said, and stepped in front of her. He had yet to physically manhandle her, but the warning in his eyes conveyed that might change if she kept pushing.

Each time she moved, he mirrored her, blocking her ability to get around him. "Get out of my way."

He pressed his lips together and shook his head. At least he had the decency to look conflicted. "They will kill you."

She blinked at his calm statement. If he had used force to stop her, she wouldn't have thought twice about leaving, but the calm way he delivered that sentence made her stop and stare at him. If the lore he believed was true, then if she died, he died.

"And then they will poison the rest of the world. That is their end game."

The gentleness of his voice was as convincing as his words, and she glanced over his shoulder at the woods. Still, she couldn't let more people die because of the Caniculas' greediness. She had already lost too much to them.

"Then come with me."

He wiped his face. "Without control over your magic, we are bound to lose."

She lifted her hand, and she willed sparks to dance across her fingers. They obeyed her silent request.

He laughed. "I know you possess it, and obviously can control it while things are calm, but I'm not sure you really want to vaporize the town if you go into panic mode like you did last night with those wolves."

She folded her hand in on itself, dousing the flames. Despite the hit to her ego, Elijah was right. She'd exploded the night before, and wiped out the wolves along with some of the trees. The blackened mark on the land that was now covered with snow was a reminder of her lack of practice. She didn't want to take that chance in town. She did not want to be a killer of the innocent.

"Then teach me how to control it." She studied his expression and how the tightness around his mouth relaxed. "But we can't wait too long, because if they are the ones doing the killing, they will get the townspeople riled up enough to come hunting for you. And Herk is an excellent tracker."

"If this Herk is a Canicula, he will not be able to breach those woods." Elijah pointed towards the barrier separating the tundra from the mountain caverns they now sat in. "The farthest he can go is the barren fields. That was the curse that I made just before the ice took my last breath. I bound *them* to the town of Opal, just as they bound me in ice."

Her eyebrows rose, and she glanced at the ground trying to recall their hunting adventures as children. Every time they got close to the outer woods, he would say he wasn't feeling well and wanted to head back. Even when she had gone into these woods with her bow, he stayed in the field instead of following her. He always seemed so envious when she came back, but she thought it was the kill she carried or dragged with her.

"Come. Sit." He waved towards the spot near the fire. "It's time to master the magic you can tap, which seems to be fire related, which may be the one thing that has saved you from falling ill to their tea."

"How so?" Lisa took a seat, and he followed, sitting close enough for her to feel the heat from his leg. She had an urge to reach out and touch him again but refrained. Petting a tiger was different than rubbing a man's leg.

"Well, tar melts under flame, and soot and ash are fire-born material, so perhaps under stress, it burned through the poison that built up over the years.”

She made a derisive noise. “It wasn’t the magic. It was having you near that allowed it to reach the surface. Herk had me training day after day for a very long time, and the only significant thing I did was roll a pencil a few inches across a table, but even that could have been attributed to the wind.”

Elijah sucked in his bottom lip as he seemed to contemplate what she’d said. “If that’s true, that means I have to be near you at all times in Opal. At least until we can identify and eradicate all the evil.”

He stood and collected some wood, then set it up in a small dip in the rock floor before returning next to her. He pointed his chin at the logs. “In the meantime, we have work to do. Start the fire, please.”

She went to stand, but he put a hand on her knee, keeping her in place. When she lifted her hand to blast the logs, he shook his head. His strong fingers clasped hers, forcing her to lower her arms. This time when she conceded, he didn’t remove his grip on hers, and she didn’t want him to.

“With your mind.” He lightly tapped her temple. “That is where your power is. Your hands are just the messenger. Your mind is where you will be able to see true evil and destroy it, so we need to strengthen that muscle." He lifted her hand. "And we may need to work on using this, too, but that will be later. Now light the fire."

"How?"

"Use your imagination. Visualize. Envision the spark and then the flame under the wood as if you just stuffed the spaces with paper and lit it with a match."

This felt way too much like Herk's training sessions, except Elijah's tone was calm and soft versus Herk's loud commands.

"Close your eyes and see it," he said, nodding at the wood. "And once you actually see it in your mind's eye, command your magic to make it so."

She studied the small wooden teepee he had built and then closed her eyes, doing exactly as he'd described. In her mind, she stuffed paper in between the logs and leaned over, striking a match. She held it to the paper until it was burning before dropping the stub left between her fingers.

A low whistle came from Elijah and Lisa opened her eyes. She hadn't just started a fire. She'd started a blaze.

Elijah smiled. "That was more controlled than last night, but you nearly made that wood explode. The fact you didn't is a step in the right direction, though. Now, control the flame," he said and pointed.

"Control it how?"

"Make it into something. Anything will do. A bird, a heart, anything. Just manipulate it." This time his voice carried some exasperation.

Lisa pressed her lips against a smile and closed her eyes. She envisioned a tiger made of flame.

"Jesus," he whispered in an alarming tone.

Her eyes popped open and widened at the mammoth flaming tiger in front of them. She slid back at the heat radiating from it. When it turned its head and snarled at the two of them, he grabbed her wrist.

The flames snuffed out completely.

Lisa looked at his hand on her wrist and then at him. Her heart thundered in her chest. She had created that thing, and somehow, just for a moment, it seemed to get away from her control.

"How did you do that?" She waved at the smoke still hanging on the air.

"I wished it so, but I had to be touching you to diffuse your magic." He smiled at her. "I cannot imagine what you would be like today if this had been allowed to be cultivated. You are most certainly the strongest elemental I have ever encountered." Interest sparkled in his blue eyes.

Lisa shifted away from him and stuffed her hands in her pockets. Again, she wondered if this man was the one she should be afraid of and not the Caniculas. Her mind drifted back to Molly and the lack of footprints leading away from her murder scene. He had some magic if he could bind the Canicula's to Opal and stop her flames from going out of control.

"Can you go from one spot to another in the snow without leaving footsteps?"

"No. I cannot wish myself from one spot to another. I am not capable of teleporting elsewhere. The only things I can do is transform into a tiger and neutralize out-of-control magic by touch. I didn't even know I was capable of creating a binding spell until I woke a couple of years ago. Unfortunately, I was not within reach of those miserable Canicula beasts when they slaughtered my soulmate and cast me in ice." He pressed his lips together and inhaled before he glanced at Lisa. "And it only took you three hundred years to bind your soul to magic and return." He let out a soft laugh.

Lisa blinked rapidly. Her mind stuck on his words, and his crooked smile did nothing to stop the chill that crawled down her spine.

"Fire and ice," he said. "I guess it is appropriate and perhaps why their poison was ineffective in squashing your gifts."

"I'm sorry. I'm having trouble understanding this. You think I'm your soulmate come back from the dead?" Had she traded one crazy for another?

He chuckled and looked down at the floor of the cavern. "This was prophesized long before either one of us were born. I did not believe it. Not until I woke up and felt the barrier protecting the rest of the world from the Caniculas. *That* was when I believed the prophecy, and I knew someday I would be standing here with you."

Lisa stared at him, unsure of what to say.

He shrugged. "I just didn't know what kind of force you would become."

While her mind rebelled against his every word, the cells in her body hummed like being this close to him was where she was meant to be. It was all too crazy, but then again, she had powers she didn't quite understand, and she needed to if she was going back into the belly of the beast.

Chapter 13

THE NEXT FEW DAYS consisted of hunting, resting, sparring, and practicing her magic. Being with Elijah had a calming effect on her. He made her feel whole again, filling that missing piece that had been gone since she had been told of her parents' death. Although his absence of vengeance against the Caniculas made her look at her own emotions.

The more she worked with Elijah, the more she trusted his version of the truth. And the more she used her magic, the more she resented the Caniculas. Elijah coached her on control, not just of magic, but of her moods and her mind as well. Only in letting go of her anger would she be able to see the true measure of their hearts.

The way to win this coming battle was not to give in to bitterness.

"Let's try something different," he said as he skinned the rabbit they had caught during their daily hunting jaunt. He put it on a cooking spike over an empty firepit and stepped away. "Tonight, I want you to try to do two things at once with your magic."

"Excuse me?" Just when she was getting comfortable with her magic, he had to throw a wrench into the mix.

"I want you to cook the rabbit for us, not charbroil it, and I want you to create a ring of fire near the entrance big enough so my tiger form can jump through. You'll need to give me enough room so I don't just jump off the ledge, though, okay?"

How in the world was that okay? She let out a laugh, like he must be joking.

"I'm serious, Lisa. You've done well with just one task, but we need to up your game before we set out for town."

"You're coming with me?"

"Don't sound so surprised. You said you thought being near me was what unleashed your magic, so I'm not taking any chances. But I will stay hidden, because I don't want them to recognize me. At least not until I can prove my innocence. Now stop sidetracking and do as I asked." He waved to the firepit and to the entry to the cavern before shifting into the beautiful tiger. His blue eyes gleamed in the semi-darkness as he waited for her to do as he'd bid.

Lisa took a deep breath to calm the sudden hammering of her heart that seeing him in tiger form always seemed to produce. She concentrated on a point on the wall between the firepit and the entrance, trying to ignore the stress crawling on her skin like a thousand fleas. If she failed, they either wouldn't eat or at the very worst, she would cook Elijah instead and end up freeing the Caniculas.

She closed her eyes and envisioned the circle first. His chuff echoed softly in the cave, and she opened her eyes to a circle she couldn't even fit her own hand through. After another cleansing breath, she willed the circle to become bigger. The fire obeyed, and she halted when the circle was almost the circumference of the cave entrance. If anyone was down below, they would think this cave was on fire. She pulled back on the inner part of the circle, leaving a space large enough for Elijah to jump through.

He did. And then turned and jumped back inside. He didn't stop like she thought he would.

He just kept jumping in and out of her flaming circle.

Lisa knew he wanted her to continue. To start the fire under the rabbit just high enough to slow roast the carcass. She tore her eyes away from Elijah and looked at the empty firepit. In the back of her mind, she kept the vision of the ring of fire intact. At the same time, she willed sparks to ignite below the rabbit. It was difficult without a source for the flame to feed on, and she pushed harder.

Elijah yelped at the same time a blaze jumped up under the rabbit, scorching the outer layer of meat. The smell of burnt rabbit and singed fur filled the cavern. She closed her eyes, dousing both flames herself without his help.

"Why did you stop?" Elijah said in a strained voice.

Lisa opened her eyes and glanced at him as he inspected the angry red burn on his arm.

"That's why," she said and crossed to him, staring at the damage she had done. "I was supposed to cook the rabbit, not you."

He smiled. "I'm only singed. And you did sear the rabbit, but it isn't charred." He piled some wood underneath the rabbit and gave her a raised brow. "But it still needs to cook a little more."

With a flick of her wrist, the wood ignited.

"What did you learn this time?" he asked as he retrieved some snow from outside and packed it on his arm.

"That I can't take my eye off of what I'm doing?"

"Well, sometimes you have to, but in most cases if you aren't fully concentrating and in control, things will go awry. You will need to split your attention at times, but you need to understand the ramifications if you can't control the magic." He held up his arm.

"I am so sorry," she said and reached out to his reddened skin.

He didn't flinch at her touch, and that fresh feeling of the air before a storm surrounded them. They both stared at the connection and then met each other's gazes. The heat that built between them caught her breath in her throat.

Elijah leaned towards her, his eyes sparkling in a way she hadn't noticed before.

A shuffle outside the cavern startled both of them. They spun to the sight of one of the children from the village. The girl's hair was matted and her face streaked with tears as she shivered in only her night shirt and socks. It was cold enough outside to be frostbite weather.

"Dear lord," Lisa whispered, and rushed to the girl. "Cheri, is that you?" she asked, scooping the girl into her arms.

The child's shakes were so bad that Lisa had no idea if she nodded or not. She moved close to the fire and grabbed her coat off the rock to wrap Cheri in it.

She rubbed Cheri's arms, trying to get the blue to recede from her fingers. "What in the world are you doing so far from home in just your nightgown?"

"He killed my family," she whispered through chattering teeth. "Slaughtered them one by one, but my momma told me to run. She said I had to find you. You would be able to stop him." Her dark eyes stared at Lisa.

"Stop who?"

Tears fell again. "The white tiger." Her gaze moved to Elijah. "But not a real tiger like I saw in here when I was climbing the mountainside. This one stalks on two legs and carries claws." She brought her gaze back to Lisa, and her chin trembled as fresh tears fell. "I saw his face."

Lisa traded a glance with Elijah. "Who killed your family?" Lisa asked, dreading the answer. She thought she knew who was doing the killing. He had been at both scenes, and she had caught a glimpse of his dark side.

"Mr. Canicula," she whispered.

"Herk?" she asked just to make sure.

Cheri shook her head. "No. Mr. Canicula."

Lisa sat back on her haunches, and a measure of relief swept through her. She had been so sure Herk had been the killer. Even with Elijah's stories of his parents, they had never been nasty to her the way Herk had been in his drunken state. She didn't know how much Herk knew, but she prayed he hadn't known of his parents' plans. She didn't think she could handle his duplicity on top of everything else.

She didn't want to hurt Herk if she didn't have to, but Mr. and Mrs. Canicula were another story. They had to be stopped at all costs.

"Have there been any other attacks since I left?" she asked Cheri.

"Mr. Canicula told the town that the white tiger is trying to weed out the fated one." She spit on the ground. "Four families with girls died before he attacked my family. He is driving everyone into a frenzy with the purpose of hunting the tiger, except he is the one doing the killing." Her face transformed into a mask of fury.

Lisa gasped and stared up at Elijah. "We have to stop them from killing anyone else."

Elijah nodded with a tight jaw. "Will you tell the town what you told us?" he asked Cheri.

Her eyes widened and she gulped, but she nodded. "If you promise to protect me," she said in a small fear-laced voice.

"With my life," Lisa said. "But we need more than just a scared child's word. We need irrefutable proof."

Her mind raced. Mr. Canicula wouldn't keep weapons in the house, especially those used in such public murders. They would be too easy to find, and his sheds were no better. He never kept those locked, so unless he had lost a few marbles, he wasn't compromising his freedom by keeping them local. She glanced out the cavern entrance while still rubbing Cheri's arms and legs.

There was one place that was far enough away from the town to be a possibility, and it was on the Opal side of the tundra. It was well within Elijah's barrier, too. The Canicula hunting cabin. And there was even a locked trunk that neither she nor Herk could ever find the key for. They were sure that was where his father kept his hunting rifles, but now she guessed that locked trunk contained something darker.

"I think I know where you might find evidence." She looked up at Elijah. "But I'll need to provide some sort of diversion so you can check it out."

"I don't want you walking into that town alone."

"I need to. And you need to take Cheri with you and keep her safe." She glanced at the girl's clothes. This wouldn't do. She couldn't let Cheri outside without proper clothing against the harsh elements. "Do you happen to have other clothes anywhere?" She started to undress. She handed Cheri her boots and pants along with her shirt, until all she stood in was the nightshirt she had on under her clothing when she'd jumped from her window.

Cheri gratefully pulled on the clothing even though it was far too big for her pre-teen body.

Elijah stared at Lisa, slowly taking her in as the wind fluttered the thermal fabric around her. He blinked and met her gaze before nodding and disappearing down a tunnel she had never ventured into. There were a couple of tunnels that led deeper into the mountain. Maybe when this whole ordeal was over, she would explore his interior domain a little more thoroughly than she had.

When he came back, he carried a beautiful fur-lined outfit that looked as if it was new, but the moment she touched it, she knew it was as old as he was. "It was my love's favorite hunting outfit," he said. "I'm not sure if they will recognize it or not, but..."

As soon as she slipped on the pants and boots, she turned and peeled off her nightshirt, then put on the matching top and cape. Arm bands and long gloves came next and when she turned, Elijah sighed so heavily that she almost took the outfit off.

When his eyes met hers, he held out a bow and quiver that with the same patterns as those on her arm bands. "You are ready, my fated one."

Chapter 14

THE SUN HADN'T YET crested the mountains, but a deep crimson hue stretched over the town like an ominous premonition. It was enough to give Lisa pause as she took stock of her little band of warriors. Cheri, looking just as scared as she had when she'd whispered the name of the man who slaughtered her family. Elijah, who was dazzling in his fur bomber jacket and black pants. And herself, who looked like some ancient Amazon queen stepping out to battle. They made an odd group, but it would have to do. She couldn't let anyone else die while they played magical games in the cave.

"Ready?" Lisa asked Cheri.

The brave girl nodded and looked up at her in awe. Lisa gave her a quick squeeze before leading them down the mountain path. They timed it so Lisa would be walking into the center of town at the time that Mr. Canicula would be rallying the crowds like he had done at the same time each day, according to Cheri.

Just before the barrier, Elijah stopped and pulled Lisa into his arms, hugging her tightly against him. "Be careful."

His embrace bathed her in warmth, and she squeezed him back. "You, too."

Lisa begrudgingly stepped away. Elijah and Cheri veered towards the Caniculas' hunting cabin, and she waited until they were out of sight before focusing all her concentration on what she was walking into. It was likely to be a witch hunt if Elijah was correct, and she prayed she wouldn't need to use the bow he had given her against the people she was prophesied to protect.

She crossed through the barrier, feeling the tingle of it now that she knew where it was. As she stepped onto the tundra, her exposed skin prickled from the cold, and her cape billowed around her. The quiet whisper of the wind was the only noise filling the valley, like nature knew a magical showdown was about to happen and was holding its breath.

She passed by Cheri's house and the bloody mess left on the snow-dusted porch. Not even Constable Jones remained. It was all as Cheri had described the last few mornings, and she knew where the town had gathered. It wasn't the town hall like she had expected. He gathered them at the great circle, using the sacred grounds to rally the crowd.

The legendary place where good would triumph against evil. Even in the Caniculas' version of the lore, this was where the white tiger would be defeated. The gathering spot where the fated one would finally light the pyre.

Mr. Canicula's voice carried over the crowd telling them the same bullshit Cheri had said he had been feeding them. As Lisa approached, the people closest to the back of the crowd glanced over their shoulders at her. Their chants silenced, and they parted, as did the rest of the group until a path cut straight to where Mr. and Mrs. Canicula were standing.

In the center of the great circle stood a single post surrounded by mounds of cut logs. Iron shackles swayed from the post like a ghost was dancing in the breeze. There was enough firewood to create a bonfire, or roast a tiger, which from Mr. Canicula's tirade was exactly what this display was for.

A hush fell over the crowd. When Mr. Canicula turned to see why silence had fallen over his minions, his voice faltered. His eyes widened at the sight of her, and she recognized fear before he had a chance to mask it.

She stopped at the opening and stared him down.

"Well, if it isn't the traitorous whore," he said and crossed his arms.

"I'm not the one slaughtering his own people," she replied.

Confusion appeared on the few faces she could see. Looks were traded, and gazes bounced from her to Mr. and Mrs. Canicula.

"She is the one responsible for the deaths in this town!" he bellowed and pointed at her. "She has never fit in and has used the prophecy for her own nefarious activities!"

The crowd turned towards her, their faces going feral. How soon they forgot she was revered as the fated one who would stop evil from overshadowing Opal.

Oh, the bastard knows how to twist a tale all right.

"Murderer!" His voice thundered over the crowd. "Grab her!"

No one moved.

A noise behind her startled her. She spun towards it, trying to get her bow off her shoulder, but she didn't have time. Herk barreled into her, knocking her to the ground. Fortunately, Elijah had practiced escape moves in various situations, and this was one of them. Herk had also made her practice this type of move once upon a time as well. She used their falling inertia to throw him over her head.

She scrambled to her feet and glanced at her bow on the ground out of reach and the arrows sprinkled around from the impact.

The crowd moved back, clearing the way for this battle of brawn versus brains. Lisa knew she didn't have a prayer without a weapon, but at least she had a few new moves up her sleeve thanks to Elijah. She set her feet in place, ready for his next attack, and kept her ears open for any attempt to blindside her in the event someone else decided to jump into the fray.

He stepped in and swung his fist. She parried, blocking the first punch, but she missed the gut shot. It was so hard that it picked her off her feet and yanked the air from her lungs.

The crowd's cheers turned to hisses when she spun away and landed a kick on the side of Herk's face. He stumbled back and cupped his cheek where she'd hit him. A playful smile formed along with a spark in his eyes. She hadn't ever landed a strike like that in the past, and it seemed to fuel whatever twistedness made Herk tick.

This time he approached more cautiously, his fists loose, matching the easy smile on his face. "You've been practicing?"

Lisa shrugged and gasped for air as her stomach throbbed. "I'm just paying attention," she said breathlessly.

His next swing grazed her cheek, but she moved quickly enough to knock him off balance. She swept his feet from under him and squared herself again, mindful of keeping her distance from anyone else.

Herk climbed to his feet and dusted himself off within striking distance, but she didn't take advantage of the open shot he gave her. When he glanced up, he cocked an eyebrow and faked to one side. But then he surprised her by tackling her full-on. He landed on top of her, and before she could twist under him and roll like she had been taught, he pinned her arms next to her head.

The crowd went wild with cheers.

"Why did you do it? Why would you kill those people?" he asked, staring down at her with confusion in his eyes.

"I didn't kill anyone." She didn't trust Herk to believe her, but she wasn't about to reveal the real culprit until she had proof. The crowd would scoff at her declaration of innocence, especially if she pointed a finger at Mr. Canicula without evidence.

Iron cuffs clasped around her wrists, and she glanced up to see Mr. Canicula's mean smile. Herk climbed to his feet as Mr. Canicula dragged Lisa to the wooden post.

"It's time to pay for your crimes," he snarled loud enough for the crowd to hear.

They cheered like this was a game. He hauled her arms up over her head and secured them to the post.

She kicked out and hit his shin, but all he did was grimace.

He stared down at her with a sneer. "I told you what I would do if you crossed me," he said in a low rumble.

The crowd chanted "Burn her" as if they had been put under some dark spell.

Herk approached. "What are you doing?" he asked his father. "You said you would put her in jail until her trial."

Lisa laughed as she kept her eye on the crowd. They were far enough back to not be able to hear their exchange, especially over the continued call for her death. "Your father's a monster."

"This *is* her trial," Mr. Canicula said and spun towards the crowd. "What say you?" he bellowed, holding his arms wide.

"Burn the witch!" they yelled, caught up in the frenzy. The noise was deafening.

"No!" Herk shouted above the crowd.

His father glared over his shoulder at him. "Shut your mouth boy and step away."

Herk stepped closer to her. "Do you have proof that she did it?" Doubt painted his features, and he glanced at her before looking at the bloodthirsty crowd surrounding them.

"Son, step away," Mrs. Canicula said softly from the side of the pyre. "She is not worth this fight."

"Says the woman who poisoned me for years with tea made of tar," Lisa said and stared down her false accusers.

Mrs. Canicula's eyes narrowed.

Lisa glanced at Herk. "Did you know?"

The shock on his face screamed innocence just as his current stance against his parents' need to destroy her. It was as if he really, truly did care for her.

"Know what?" He eyed the restless crowd from his place next to her on their makeshift bonfire kindling.

"That her black tea was actually poison meant to kill my magic and eventually kill me," she said.

"She said it was special to help you tap magic if you had it." His wide grey gaze met hers before it shot to his mother. "And that's why I could never have any."

"Herk, step away," she said, her features hardened. "Now."

He looked back at her, his eyes pleading, but for what she had no idea.

"I've never lied to you," Lisa whispered. "Even when I knew what I had to say would hurt."

"We can't just publicly execute her!" he shouted over the crowd's chant.

"Sure, we can," Mr. Canicula snarled, "and if you don't get off this pyre, I'll just burn you right along with her."

Mrs. Canicula's face registered the same shock Lisa felt.

"Randolph, please," Mrs. Canicula begged.

He glared and pointed at her. "This is your doing."

"Don't hurt him," she whispered, pleading.

"Then get him off this wood stack before I set it on fire."

"Herk, come down here now," Mrs. Canicula said and held out her hand.

Herk looked at his mother and then back at Lisa. He shook his head. "This isn't right. This isn't following the law like you've always preached," he argued.

His father grabbed his wrist and shackled him as well. "You fool."

While some still chanted, others stopped at the new development. All eyes were glued to the scene before them. It was not only their perceived murderer, but now it was the Canicula's son on the pyre.

Mr. Canicula stepped off the wood pile and lit a match, but before he could toss it on the wood, Mrs. Canicula blocked him.

"Please," she pleaded, but his stare was colder than the midnight wind.

"Father?" Herk pulled at his bound wrists.

"I am not your father," he snapped and pushed Mrs. Canicula aside. "Your mother fucked a human." His gaze moved to Lisa. "Your father slept with my wife long before he met your mother. The bastard ran before I had a chance to skin him alive. Too bad the fool came back to Opal."

Lisa's blood chilled. In so many words, Mr. Canicula had admitted to killing her father. She sucked air in between her teeth, containing the sudden swell of fury that clawed at the surface. She glanced at Herk, and for the first time, noticed that his eyes were the same shade of grey as hers. The same shade as her father's.

This wasn't another lie. She could see the devastating truth in Mrs. Canicula's eyes as Mr. Canicula threw the match.

She had a brother. The thought struck her hard as the match traveled through the air and landed on the wood.

"What are you doing?" Herk cried and pulled at the chains holding him to the post.

The crowd gasped and cheered as the wood burst into flame in more of an explosion than a slow burn as if Mr. Canicula had treated it with an accelerant.

Mrs. Canicula threw herself forward, but Mr. Canicula caught her around the waist and pulled her to safety. Still, she wailed at the sight of her son in mortal peril.

Heat filled the space around them, and Lisa closed her eyes, leaning her head against the wood post. Herk yanked at the chain holding him in place, pleading for help, but there was no help coming from Opal.

She was the only one who could get them out of this predicament, and they had chosen fire to try to destroy her. Fire. Her chosen element. She smiled.

The first thing she needed to address were the chains. She couldn't hold the fire at bay forever, and being bound in the middle of the danger zone wouldn't fare well for either of them if she lost control of it. Iron could melt and that is what she concentrated on. Heating the cuffs to the point their structural integrity wasn't enough to keep them bound.

The burn of hot metal made her wince, but in a matter of moments, the cuffs holding her in place were weak enough for her to tear her hands from. She grabbed Herk's arm and yanked, despite his howling.

He just stared at her and grasped his wrist.

In the distance, a tiger charged towards them surrounded by children. And even through the wall of flames obstructing most of her view, she saw the panic in Elijah's eyes.

Herk went to move, and she grabbed his arm. "Don't run."

She concentrated on pushing the flames to the edge of the wood pile. It still blazed high enough for people to step back. Mr. Canicula held Mrs. Canicula against his chest and smiled in triumph at the wall of flames. Lisa could see him, but he couldn't see through the block she'd created.

"Are you—"

"Shush," she interrupted Herk.

When she thought she had total control of the blaze, she looked beyond them at the Caniculas and willed the fire to encircle them. The fire obeyed, trapping them in a circle of flame before they understood what was happening. Gasps came from the crowd, almost making Lisa's control falter.

"We need to get off this wood," she said as sweat dripped from her forehead. She kept her hands splayed and her focus on the fire ring.

Herk gently took her arm and kept her steady as he helped navigate them from the pile. When they reached the ground, he let go of her.

"Do not harm the tiger," she yelled without breaking her concentration. "The only thing about the lore we've all been fed over the years that is true is that the fated one would rid Opal of evil. The tiger is *not* evil!"

"But..."

"She's right," Cheri said, stepping into the crowd. She threw a bloodied fake claw on the ground in front of Constable Jones.

He gasped. "We thought you were dead."

"That's exactly what Mr. Canicula wanted everyone to think about all of us." Cheri waved at the other children surrounding the tiger. "That was in Mr. Canicula's hunting cabin along with the other kids."

"The tiger has put them under a spell," Mr. Canicula yelled, but his words had an empty effect on the crowd.

"Shut up!" Herk snapped venomously and pointed a finger at him. "You were willing to burn me to a crisp because I wanted due process for Lisa. You chose to be judge and jury and sentence innocent people to death. So just shut your mouth."

Some of the flames shot back to the pyre before she could harness them again, and Lisa gave Herk a side-eye.

"I saw the man who killed my family!" Cheri pointed towards the circle of flame holding the Canicula's prisoners. "He slaughtered my family with that thing." She nodded towards the bloody man-made claw. "Mr. and Mrs. Canicula are the real monsters in this town."

Even Constable Jones seemed frozen with indecision.

The townspeople were no better. Just like Herk, they seemed to be grappling with the poison they had been fed for generations. And they all seemed to be looking to Herk for direction.

No one knew quite what to do now that the white tiger was here and not living up to the expectations painted for centuries.

Herk looked down at the bloodied man-made paw as well as the pristine one another child held. Both looked rudimentary. He pointed to the one that another little girl named Mary held. "Press the end in the snow."

Mary did as Herk asked. When she pulled it out, she said, "Mr. Canicula killed my family, too and he and Mrs. Canicula came to the cabin and killed Tommy and Joe. They drank their blood," she said and scrunched her face. "And then told us we were next."

Lisa clenched her fists, and the fire flared brighter. It took her a moment to get it back under control. Luckily it didn't devour Mr. and Mrs. Canicula. She was not the judge and jury and would not be the one to take justice into her own hands, even if that was what she wanted to do.

Herk wiped his face and paled as he stared at the pristine tiger footprint. "Where in the cabin did you find this?" he asked Cheri.

"The locked trunk."

"If it was locked, how did you get it open?"

While Herk seemed unconvinced by the evidence and even his parents' actions, Lisa knew better. Herk asked lots of questions when his mind was having trouble reconciling the truth in front of him with his feelings. She was sure this was as much of a loop as it was for her.

"He picked the lock," Cheri said and pointed at the tiger.

The children seemed to move closer, each putting their hand on his fur in both a protective and grateful manner.

"Cheri found us in the caverns. She ran all the way there in her nightshirt," Lisa said, knowing he would understand just how frightened this child must have been to flee without winter protection.

He stared at her and then glanced at his parents.

"Don't believe that lying witch," Mr. Canicula snarled.

"The hunting cabin was the only place I could think of where your father had a place to hide things. And we never could figure out where the key to that trunk was," she added softly, bringing up memories of their childhood adventures in the woods while he processed everything.

He swiped his hand down his face, and Lisa could tell that the past few minutes were spinning in his head by the way his eyes seemed to widen as he stared at the bloody man-made paw. His gaze lifted to the white tiger in the center of the group of children, and his gaze narrowed. He took a wobbling step towards the beast.

Lisa grabbed his arm, steadying him the way he had helped her when they climbed off the wood pile meant to be their death. She had always felt a connection to Herk, always thought of him as a big brother, which was why his proposal threw her so hard, and even now as he stood debating on his loyalties, she felt that connection.

"Don't do anything stupid, brother," she said, keeping the lion's share of her focus on the ring of fire burning around his parents.

He stared into her eyes for a long time. "He tried to kill me."

She nodded.

Herk turned to his parents. "Lock them up. Their trial starts tomorrow."

Lisa snuffed out the flame and Constable Jones and his deputies descended on Mr. and Mrs. Canicula like flies on spoiled meat.

Chapter 15

LISA SAT ON THE couch in one of the empty homes near the town center with both her arms bandaged. The burns from the melting iron still itched and would be a reminder of this entire ordeal. The six orphaned children, including Cheri, sat on the floor with crayons and paper, coloring as they waited for the sentencing of Mr. and Mrs. Canicula.

The past few days had been reveal after reveal of the atrocities the Caniculas had delivered to Opal over the centuries. From the burning of Elijah's love at the same stake they had tried to sacrifice Lisa and Herk on, to the slaughtering of families over the years, including Lisa's parents and grandparents.

Mrs. Canicula had cooperated. Spilling truth after ugly truth, including poisoning Lisa with tar-tea to destroy the magic inside her. She didn't know why it didn't work. And all throughout her testimony, Mr. Canicula glared at her from the defendant's box.

The most damning evidence was the children's testimonies. They didn't divert from one another. Each one witnessed their parents' death and then Mr. Canicula swept them away to the cottage, tying them up for his amusement. They were vampires alright, and with the children, they chose to make their deaths a display of blood and gluttony.

Lisa's stomach had churned and almost spilled their contents at the description. She looked at the children, silently admiring their bravery for facing those vampiric monsters.

Elijah stepped into the doorway leading to the kitchen. "Breakfast is ready."

Crayons were dropped, and a flurry of arms and legs filled the space as everyone ran to the kitchen table. Lisa followed and stopped next to Elijah, watching as the children climbed up on chairs and started helping themselves to bacon and eggs that Elijah had whipped up.

"Are you okay?" he asked and brushed a piece of hair out of her face.

She shook her head. "Not particularly."

The Caniculas had been found guilty on all counts. If sentenced to death, it would be her duty to annihilate them with her magic. Which meant death by fire, and that was never pretty or humane.

A knock at the door interrupted them and she crossed to open it. Herk stood on the other side, his face drawn with exhaustion. Finding out he was the son of an immortal had seemed just as hard as his father's betrayal.

He was flanked by two officers, and his arms were behind his back.

"Death." He grimaced as he said that lone word. Then he met her gaze.

Lisa swallowed hard.

He let out a little laugh. "They aren't sparing me either."

She blinked and her eyes widened.

Herk didn't do anything. Why are they sentencing him to death?

"What?" she asked to make sure she'd heard him right.

"Guilty by association. Monster blood and all." He shrugged a shoulder.

Her gaze hardened, and she shook her head. She turned toward Elijah. "This is not right—" She waved at Herk in the doorway. "—He did nothing wrong."

Elijah's open jaw was enough to announce his equal shock at the sentencing. "But he's innocent."

She looked back at Herk and the guards holding him hostage. She couldn't let this happen. "Killing an innocent man is not part of the deal."

"I'm sorry, Miss Winters, but the jury demanded the complete destruction of the Canicula bloodline."

"And what of the Winters' bloodline?" she asked and stormed out the door past the guards.

She marched towards where the crowd was forming. This town seemed to have a taste for public executions, and it had to stop. It was as if the Caniculas had truly destroyed the humanity of this little town.

She made her way through the crowd until she stood before three posts and more wood piled than before. The middle post was empty, but Mr. and Mrs. Canicula were bound to the other two and struggling in their bonds.

When the guards with Herk went to pass her, she put her hand out. Flames licked her fingers.

"Do not go any farther," she said. "He is not one of them. He is my half brother."

"But he is also a Canicula," the judge said from her station to the right of the pyre. "And therefore must be eliminated."

Chants of "burn them" started behind her, and she realized the Caniculas' evil had spread to the human hearts of this community.

"Herk is not evil. I will not abide by this ruling." She turned towards the crowd as the chants continued.

The frenzied looks in their eyes saddened her, and when Elijah stepped into her sight in tiger form, his eyes magnified her despair.

"My job as the fated one is to rid Opal of evil." A tear escaped, sending a hot path down her cheek. "What I see and hear before me is evil." She choked on her words. "This bloodlust is evil." Tears now flowed freely as her voice echoed above the chants.

She turned towards the pyre and pointed. "They are not the only ones who harbor evil in their hearts. If you cannot recognize it in your own soul, there is no hope for Opal."

Only a few catcalls of "Burn them!" remained. The rest of the crowd looked shamed at their actions.

"Justice is not the same as bloodlust. Executing Mr. and Mrs. Canicula is just. Executing Herk makes you no better than them." She pointed behind her at the pyre. "I am willing to be the hand of justice, but I will not murder an innocent man because of your unfounded fear." She gave one last glance at the crowd before turning to the judge. "Rethink your sentence."

The judge recoiled, her face reddened and scrunched in anger. "The judgement stands."

Lisa clenched her fists. Magic swelled inside her, and she met Herk's gaze, shaking her head slowly before she closed her eyes. The tiger roared, but she ignored him. Evil must be annihilated, and the innocent must be protected.

"Justice," she whispered and concentrated.

White light filled her vision and all she saw were human hearts. Nearly a dozen of them were blackened and shriveled, including the judge's, but the multitude of them carried vessels filled with the light of hope.

Screams filled the air along with gasps. She opened her eyes, and the people with evil shriveling their hearts became human torches in the crowd. Lisa turned towards the pyre. Mr. and Mrs. Canicula smiled at the pandemonium, drinking it all in until they realized Lisa was looking at them.

Lisa only saw the root of evil blackened and sickened within these two monsters. Fire leapt from her, sweeping forward like a wave, leaving only ash floating on the air where the Caniculas had once been bound. Not even the iron shackles remained.

Herk's wide eyes stared at her. She turned back to the crowd now bathed in ash. Wind swirled and Elijah stepped from the grey mist. He started running towards her, and she couldn't understand the horror in his gaze.

When he was close, he leapt through the air, turning into the tiger before he hit her, slamming her down to the ground with the force of his weight. She smelled singed fur just before everything went black.

Hushed whispers surrounded her, penetrating the blackness, but Lisa could not make out the words, nor could she escape the darkness pulling her into oblivion.

Chapter 16

A COOL DAMPNESS CARESSED her forehead. Lisa moaned and tried to open her eyes, but her lids seemed crusted closed. She lifted her hand to wipe them, but a cloth swiped across her eyes instead.

"Shhh," a deep voice softly cooed and then that heavenly dampness wiped her eyes again.

She blinked them open but couldn't quite see clearly. It took her a few blinks to focus on the face hovering over her. Blue eyes peered down from a face that held deep creases of concern.

"You scared us all for a spell." Elijah continued wiping her face and neck with the cloth before dipping it into a bucket next to the bed she was laid out on.

"What happened?" she whispered with a voice hoarse and raspy.

"You became the hand of justice smiting evil. It was something to behold." He smiled, but his concern still hung on the air. He kept methodically wiping her face and neck with the cool cloth that smelled of honey and peppermints. His lips held tightness even though he tried to smile for her.

"What aren't you telling me?" she asked after another swipe of coolness.

His smile faded and he sighed. "I didn't react as fast as I should have." He closed his eyes for a moment and then went back to washing her gently with the cloth.

She lifted one of her hands and stared at the bandages covering her skin. What she saw was red and angry with patches of blisters poking out from under the gauze. Her last memory of singed fur surfaced, and she looked closer at him. His arms had bandages that looked like those on her hands, and her gaze jumped to his.

"I burned you?"

He sighed. "Rest. You're pretty doped up on medicine right now, and you need the sleep." He gave her a grimace of a smile.

"But you're hurt," she said and started to sit up. Every muscle protested with a scream of pain, and she fell back.

"I'm fine." He swiped her shoulder and arm with the cloth. "But we nearly lost you." This time when his gaze met hers, tears glossed his eyes. He swallowed and closed his eyes for a moment before looking back at her. "The doctor should be back to check on us in a little while."

She relaxed back into the bed and glanced around at their surroundings. Her heart lurched in her chest at the metal bars surrounding them.

"Jail?"

His smile softened. "This was the only place they could really sterilize to address our wounds. The doors aren't locked, and there hasn't been anyone in the jail for a while. We can control infection better here than at the doctor's office or someone's home."

A throat cleared from behind Elijah. He turned and Herk appeared at his side.

"Hey," he said. The side of his face looked like he had fallen asleep in the sun.

Lisa's stomach dropped. "I hurt you, too?"

His hand jumped to his face. "Nothing more than a sunburn," he said with a nervous laugh. "Most of us who were near you ended up like this, but it will eventually clear up." He crossed and took a seat at the foot of her bed.

"What else is happening out there?"

Herk looked over his shoulder at the open doorway and sighed. "The townsfolk are somewhere between awed and scared." He locked gazes with her. "They keep coming to me like I have answers." He shook his head. "I don't know how to put people at ease. I just know how to beat the crap out of people. Or run them ragged until they tell me to..." He looked at her pointedly.

"Sod off?" she said and snorted laughter.

He smiled. "I think I've come to terms with you being my little sister. It certainly explains my insane need to push you and protect you at the same time."

"So, you agree you were being unreasonable?"

Elijah's lips formed a smirk, and he raised an eyebrow at her as he wiped her other arm with the salve.

Herk glanced at Elijah and then back at her. "Considering what you actually did, I don't think I was being unreasonable at all. I just didn't know my mother was poisoning you." He looked down at his hands. "I had some time to talk to her alone. She didn't want to talk at first, but I told her she owed it to me considering I was sentenced to death alongside her, just for being her son. She opened up. Told me about her affair with our father. She said he was kind and pure-hearted, just like you are. And he didn't shy away from her when she told him what she was. He asked a lot of questions, so you have a great deal of him in you, but when Randolph found out, she made your dad leave town. He never knew my mother was pregnant."

That did sound like her father. He always told her to question everything because that was the only way to get to the truth. She nodded.

"When you and your family came back, it devastated my mother. Your dad had given his whole heart to your mother, and the minute you stepped into town, my father knew magic had intruded on Opal and the prophecy was imminent unless he could change it in some way. He apparently wanted to kill you right then and there, along with your parents, but my mom couldn't abide killing the child of someone she cared a great deal for. Although, she gave my father some bullshit excuse that worked because..." He waved halfheartedly at her.

"I guess I am glad she had a heart," Lisa said.

He nodded. "I'm glad, too. Although I wish she had clued me in before I made a royal ass out of myself with you."

"You didn't know. It was kind of creepy because I just couldn't get past seeing you like a brother."

"Thank god," he said and shivered at what might have transpired had Lisa said yes to him. "Anyway, it seems every day was a battle for my mother to keep you alive. It wasn't until I showed interest that my father backed off because he thought that was how we would be freed. She didn't know when he figured out I wasn't his son. He manipulated us all. He knew I would have done anything to keep Opal safe, even try to go after the tiger with you. Which, according to Elijah, would have killed me if I forcefully tried to go through the barrier. So..."

"He wanted you just as dead as he wanted us," Lisa said.

"Apparently." Herk chewed the side of his lip. "When that failed, he fed me doubts about you and seeded the thought that you might be the one killing people here especially when you pointed out the lack of animal footprints around Molly and then told me the tiger didn't do this." He glanced at Elijah. "I thought you had some magical ability to pop in and attack and then be gone." He laughed under his breath. "But that's beside the point. I guess what I'm trying to say is

I'm sorry I ever doubted you." He met Lisa's gaze.

"I'm sorry I ever thought you were a part of this," she said and tried to sit up.

"Lay your ass back down," he snapped at her and then pointed at Elijah, acting more like the Herk she was used to. "Make sure she rests."

"You can count on that," Elijah said and continued to administer salve to her exposed burns.

"We'll have to figure out this sister-brother thing when you are better, but I've got to say, having a tiger as your protector is actually pretty cool." He stood and glanced at Elijah. "And he seems pretty fond of you," he added before he wandered out of the room.

She yawned, exhausted from the conversation, and met Elijah's gaze. "I'm pretty fond of you, too."

This time his smile was more natural, more dazzling. "We will have to explore this mutual fondness a little more when you are back on your feet."

"Oh, you can count on that!" She smiled and closed her eyes, wishing she could experience Elijah's kiss.

It was as if he had read her mind. His soft lips pressed down on hers, and the connection created a warm heat in the center of her heart. Sparks danced on the back of her eyelids, and her entire body tingled. This was something that could become all consuming.

She wrapped a bandaged arm around his neck and opened her mouth to deepen the kiss.

He pulled away with a chuckle, and she opened her eyes to his bright blue ones that held the same spark igniting inside her.

"Rest and heal first," he whispered in a voice that had turned husky with need. He ran his thumb across her bottom lip and smiled. "That was just a tiny incentive, so you get better as fast as humanly possible."

That was one hell of a stroke of motivation.

That little peck was not nearly enough for Lisa. She wanted so much more from her white tiger.

She wanted forever.

The End

About J.E. Taylor

J.E. Taylor is a USA Today bestselling author, a publisher, an editor, a manuscript formatter, a mother, a wife, a business analyst, and a Supernatural fangirl. Not necessarily in that order. She first sat down to seriously write in February of 2007 after her daughter asked:

"Mom, if you could do anything, what would you do?"

From that moment on, she hasn't looked back.

Besides being co-owner of Novel Concept Publishing, Ms. Taylor also moonlights as a Senior Editor of Allegory E-zine, an online venue for Science Fiction, Fantasy and Horror, and co-host of the popular YouTube talk show Spilling Ink.

She lives in New Hampshire with her husband and during the summer months enjoys her weekends on the shore in southern Maine.

Visit her at <u>www.jetaylor75.com</u> to check out her
other titles.